Valegro
Goes International

The Blueberry Stories: Book Four

Carl Hester MBE FBHS with Janet Rising
with illustrations by Helena Öhmark

Matador
9 Priory Business Park,
Wistow Road, Kibworth Beauchamp,
Leicestershire. LE8 0RX
Tel: 0116 279 2299
Email: books@troubador.co.uk
Web: www.troubador.co.uk/matador
Twitter: @matadorbooks

ISBN 978 1788037 860

British Library Cataloguing in Publication Data.
A catalogue record for this book is available from the British Library.

Printed and bound in the UK by TJ International, Padstow, Cornwall
Typeset in 12pt Book Antiqua by Troubador Publishing Ltd, Leicester, UK

Matador is an imprint of Troubador Publishing Ltd

This book is dedicated to Rowena Luard,
a dedicated owner and supporter

Chapter One

"Where are we?" Blueberry asked his travelling companion Dez.

"I don't know, but it's cold," the bright chestnut replied.

The horses had travelled from their home, Brook Mill Stables, in the comfortable horsebox, munching hay and glancing out of the high windows at the changing scenery. First the green and brown ploughed fields of Gloucestershire

1

through the driving January rain, then the grey of the motorways in dusk before the gloom of the Channel Tunnel as they sped on under the sea towards Europe on the smooth train, its engines humming like a swarm of bees. On reaching France, the horsebox was driven off the train, bowling along more motorways in darkness. Dez was right, it was cold and Blueberry was glad of his quilted rug keeping his clipped body warm, and the thick bandages around his legs.

Eventually they arrived at their destination and the little brown horse was led down the ramp by his groom, Lydia, to a large loosebox with a deep bed of wood chippings. It was almost like home – especially when Lydia had filled his water buckets and hung his haynet. She checked him over, replacing his bandages after giving his legs a rub and offering him an apple, which Blueberry accepted. He could hear Dez munching in the stable next door and when everyone had finally left them for the night, they chatted again.

"We're in Holland," said Dez, "somewhere called Zwolle. I overheard Lydia talking to Carl. Our tests are the day after tomorrow, so good luck!"

Holland! Blueberry felt a shiver of excitement. He had been born in Holland so it was always a special place for him. He thought

2

the way the people were speaking sounded familiar. He wondered whether he would recognise any of the horses competing in the competition tomorrow – perhaps one or two he had known as a foal or a youngster would be here. He never imagined he might one day travel back and compete in his home country. How exciting it was to be a dressage horse, he thought. It was such an interesting job; not only did he learn something new in every lesson, and enjoy working to improve all the movements he was asked for, but competing meant he led such an interesting life, the life he always dreamed he would live. He never knew where he would be going next, who he would be going with or who he would meet. Usually he travelled to shows with Uthopia, the almost-black stallion, but today he was with Dez, the handsome chestnut who belonged to Charlotte.

Blueberry knew Charlotte would be in his own saddle in the competition – they had trained for a long time now, and it was always Charlotte who partnered him in his dressage tests. It was strange that he was always ridden by Charlotte but on this occasion, at this competition, Charlotte's own horse, Dez, would be ridden by Carl, who owned Blueberry! He, Carl and Charlotte were a team – a good team. Blueberry had been disappointed when he realised

Carl, who he idolised and loved, wouldn't be competing him throughout his dressage career. He had always dreamed that he and Carl would be partners in competitions but Carl had thought the little brown horse too small for him to compete with. Carl had been determined to find the perfect rider to take Blueberry to the top in his dressage career. He had found her, and now Blueberry and Charlotte had reached an incredible understanding. With Carl's training and mentoring, the pair were improving all the time, enjoying their work together, working as one to improve all the difficult movements dressage horses and their riders perform and demonstrate to the judges to prove they are in harmony and balance with each other, and had trained correctly to classical tradition.

Blueberry knew that each component of the team was vital. It was his job to perform the movements with power, grace and precision; Charlotte's task was to ride beautifully and correctly, and give him the tiniest, invisible signals to let him know which movement to carry out, at which point, with the right amount of power and speed. Carl was the third element, the teacher, the coach, the mentor, there to ensure they were working in the correct way, planning their competitive careers so that they were not only successful, but that they met every competition at the peak of their ability, the peak of their training, enabling them to progress to the very top.

Of course, there were a great many other vital people who worked behind the scenes with them, and Blueberry knew that top dressage horses were never successful without a huge army of support. It was, as his friend Lulu had often told him, as though he, Charlotte and Carl were at the very peak of a pyramid, with lots of other people in the pyramid base, holding them up and helping them along. Lulu, his short-legged, tan-coloured, one-eyed friend was resident top dog at Carl's yard, and she had a way of explaining things to Blueberry that helped him make sense of the world. Blueberry wished his friend was with him now. Although she often travelled with him to shows at home, she never came to the ones abroad. He didn't know why that was, but it was always so.

"Are you looking forward to your tests tomorrow?" Blueberry asked Dez, who wasn't usually very talkative, unlike his friend Orange, but he was friendly enough.

"I am, actually," Dez replied. "I'm looking forward to competing with Carl. When he's riding me I feel I can do just about anything – which is fortunate as it will be my first Grand Prix. I think Carl is riding me because Charlotte

5

hasn't ridden at Grand Prix yet and Carl can give me some help."

Blueberry knew that feeling. He had always felt that way with Carl in his saddle, but now he was feeling it more and more with Charlotte. He loved their time together, whether schooling or competing. They had, just as Carl had predicted when he had first paired them together, gelled into a formidable partnership. How much further they could progress depended on how hard they all worked, and how much they wanted the success only hard work, ambition and talent could bring.

Blueberry realised how tired he was after the journey and he locked up a hind leg, lowered his head and closed his eyes. Thank goodness, he thought, just before nodding off to sleep, he didn't mind travelling. Some horses hated it – his friend Orange always felt tense and out of sorts whenever he had to go in the horsebox or stay away from home – but Blueberry didn't mind at all. He enjoyed seeing new places and meeting new people and horses, not to mention the chance to show everyone his paces, movements and training. The little brown horse looked forward to doing just that tomorrow. He was living his own dream – competing as a top dressage horse. Ever since he had gone to live at

Carl's yard and seen the dressage horses show

off their paces, it had always been Blueberry's dream to copy them, and fulfilling that dream was no disappointment. Nothing made him happier.

The tests were indoors, in a huge arena with enthusiastic and knowledgeable spectators keen to see which top riders had brought their young horses for experience and confidence – just as Carl and Charlotte had brought Blueberry and Dez. The dressage world is always keen to see which new horses are the ones to watch for the future. Would the people who had come today be lucky enough to see a future World or Olympic champion at the start of their international career?

Since the previous September, at the National Dressage Championships at home, Blueberry had been particularly excited and had worked harder than ever. It had been after he had won the National Prix St Georges Championship with Charlotte that Carl had gone on record as saying that he was aiming the partnership for the 2012 Olympic Games due to be held in London. Ever since Lulu had explained about the Games, how they were the ultimate test for any athlete, human or equine, how they were held only every four years and brought together the very best riders and horses from all over the world, Blueberry had wondered whether he could ever be good enough to be chosen. Only after Carl's public declaration that he was training the little brown horse and his rider Charlotte for London 2012, had Blueberry truly believed he had what it took to fulfil Carl's faith in him. At least, he had decided then, he would in two years' time, when Carl's training programme and campaign to get him and Charlotte to the Games had been completed.

"Don't think it will be easy," Lulu had warned him. She was always good at keeping his hooves on the ground when Blueberry's imagination took off into space. "Even if everything goes to plan, even if you and Charlotte prove to be good enough, you still have to be selected. The selectors decide who goes to the Games and usually there are some disappointed partnerships because not everyone can go. It isn't like a normal competition, you know. And even then," Lulu had continued, "if you do prove to be the best of the best, you still need luck on your side."

"But Carl says we make our own luck," Blueberry had said. "He says the harder we work, the luckier we become because we leave nothing to chance."

"And that's true," Lulu had agreed. "But sometimes bad luck can change things – a horse or a rider can become ill or be injured, for example, leaving the selectors no choice but to replace a promising horse and rider with another combination which is fit and able to compete."

Blueberry hadn't thought of that. He was extra careful in the field after Lulu had told him about the selectors. It wouldn't do for him to slip on the mud and hurt himself, or get kicked accidentally when he and Orange bucked and leapt about in high spirits. He couldn't imagine how awful it would be to be left behind when the Games were on just because of a stupid injury which he could have avoided.

At this competition in Zwolle, Charlotte and Carl made sure Blueberry was warmed up and worked-in with plenty of time to go before his test. They knew from experience that he was always so eager to show off his training he could be too keen in a test and spoil his chances by his exuberance. Blueberry was particularly fresh at Zwolle because of the cold, and it took some time to ensure he was relaxed and listening completely to his rider. It was important that he was mentally – as well as physically – ready for his test.

As he entered the arena for the Prix St Georges, Blueberry heard the commentator call out Charlotte's name – the only name he understood as he had forgotten most of his

9

Dutch words and was now thinking in English. He heard his own name called, too, *Valegro* – his professional name, rather than his stable name, Blueberry, given to him because all the horses which had arrived at Carl's yard that year had been named after fruit and vegetables. Orange had been the obvious choice for his chestnut friend and the little brown horse with a bluish tint to his coat had become Blueberry. He settled down to his test – which went well, he could feel it. His extravagant trot and his bouncy, long-striding canter, for which he was famous, impressed the judges. His transitions were smooth, his carriage exemplary and he felt that nothing had gone wrong. He and Charlotte had been in total harmony and all the movements had been performed well and had begun at precisely the exact spot they were supposed to.

Blueberry's instinct was right and their test was so good, the pair's high score saw them in second place. It was a brilliant result for a young horse, especially as Carl had entered them for international experience rather than with the aim of winning. It is a big step-up to go from competitions at home to those abroad in the company of international riders and horses, and coming second to a famous and experienced rider and horse was no mean feat. Travelling to new venues abroad can cause horses and riders to lose their concentration, but that didn't happen to Blueberry or Charlotte. Not for the first time Carl was impressed by both his pupils, equine and human.

Blueberry loved the whole experience – and being in the line up was particularly exciting for him. He knew by now that he performed his best when there were lots of people watching him – the bigger the crowd, the better. It was as though an invisible presence rippled through the audience, lifting his performance and willing him on to do his best. When that happened it was as though he and his rider could read each other's minds, knowing exactly what they had to do, even before any aids were given.

Their performance had been noticed by some top people.

"Did you know you're riding one of the best young horses Wim Ernes has ever seen at that level?" Carl asked Charlotte, as she steered Blueberry out of the arena after the prize-giving.

Blueberry pricked up his ears. He didn't know who Wim Ernes was, but it was obvious that Carl thought a great deal of his judgement, and it seemed to mean a lot to Charlotte, too, if her wide smile was anything to go by. It somehow made up for the fact that he had stood second, rather than first in the competition. Nobody seemed to mind that he hadn't won –

they were all delighted – but Blueberry minded. He remembered Lulu had once told him that he possessed competitive spirit, and supposed that was what she had meant. He hated losing. Not that coming second was really losing, it just wasn't quite good enough in Blueberry's mind, and a tiny part of him felt disappointed.

But Wim Ernes thought he was one of the best young horses he had ever seen at Prix St Georges level and that, Blueberry thought, seemed a good thing. His thoughts drifted to the impressive metal statue which lived on Carl's lawn outside his house, The Silver Dancer, depicted forever in the perfect piaffe, Blueberry's inspiration. His ambition was to be like that, to be a horse people remembered, the best dressage horse the world had ever seen. Even The Silver Dancer had needed to start somewhere, he thought. Had the real Silver Dancer, the one on which the metal statue had been based, had he been one of the best young horses a top dressage person had ever seen?

"People are starting to talk about Valegro as an up-and-coming star," Carl whispered in his ear, "And I've heard other people comment on how exciting a prospect you are," he added, not wanting the little brown horse to be in any way downhearted by his second place. Blueberry was happy. He had enjoyed his test, Charlotte and Carl were pleased with him and he had not only received a compliment from an important person in dressage, but other people had noticed him, too. He looked forward to his next competition, and his next audience!

Chapter Two

Back at Brook Mill, Blueberry couldn't wait to tell everyone what Wim Ernes had said about him. Orange was suitably impressed.

"Wow," said the big chestnut horse as they grazed in the field. "That's amazing. Did he really say that?"

"Yes, Carl said he did, so it must be true."

"Congratulations," said Orange, grateful

he hadn't had to go to Zwolle. From what Blueberry told him, there had been lots of people watching the tests and Orange hated being watched. He found the pressure of competitions at best trying, and at worst highly stressful. Schooling was no bother, he loved it, he enjoyed learning new things and improving his dressage movements but competitions were something else. Orange always complained that competitions were the worst thing about being a dressage horse. Blueberry couldn't help thinking that his friend had rather missed the point of being a competitive dressage horse. For him, the competitions were what all the training was about. Lulu always said it took all sorts and that everyone's motivation differed. Blueberry wasn't quite sure what she meant by that, but didn't like to ask at the time because he had already asked so many questions that day and didn't want to look stupid. Although, thinking back on it later, he decided that if Lulu didn't already think him a bit dim now, one more question was unlikely to have tipped the balance.

Blueberry told the other horses about Wim Ernes. They politely said how nice it was for him but little else. They preferred to eat grass, concentrate on their schooling or relax under the heat lamps of the solarium while Blueberry

15

was tied up next to them, bending their ears about Zwolle.

Noticing the yard cats, Bonnie and Clyde, sitting on the wall around the tree in the yard outside his stable, Blueberry told them about Wim Ernes, too. They were bound to be impressed, he thought. But far from being even interested, Bonnie emitted a quiet contemptible hiss before running across the yard to the hay barn to look for mice and Clyde, the ginger male cat, stopped licking his front paw only to stare at him with his amber eyes.

"Who?" he asked, his eyes glazed with disinterest.

"The famous Dutch dressage person, Wim Ernes," Blueberry said, glad the cat had asked. He wasn't really surprised that Clyde hadn't heard of Wim Ernes – Blueberry himself hadn't until a few days ago.

"Okay," said Clyde, sounding bored. "Is that a big deal?"

"Well, yes, it is really," said Blueberry, slightly disappointed with Clyde's reaction. He had been feeling very bouncy and excited since returning from Zwolle and the disinterested reaction of his friends, apart from Orange who had been enthusiastic, at his news hadn't matched his mood. Maybe, he thought to himself, he was telling the wrong people. He

16

supposed Clyde just wasn't really into dressage, even given where he lived.

He knew who would be impressed, though.

"My, my," said Lulu, opening her one eye wide in mock admiration at the news, "did you find your headcollar had to be let out a hole or two on the way back from Holland?"

Blueberry looked at her in puzzlement and felt his chin twitch. It tended to wobble when things didn't quite make sense in his head.

"No," he said, slowly, wondering whether he was missing something. "I don't think so. Why would it?"

"Oh, I just wondered whether it still fitted you, what with your head being so swollen and all," explained Lulu, sitting down on the yard and leaning against Blueberry's stable door, one hind foot sticking out at an angle from under her.

"Swollen?" asked Blueberry, confused. "Is it swollen?" Turning around he tried to see his reflection in the water in his automatic drinker, but it was too small. Did that mean his head *had* swollen? If he had looked in the automatic drinker last week, would his head have fitted in the reflection?

"It's the same size… I think," said Blueberry, not quite sure. "Do you think it looks swollen?"

"It's just that you sound very big-headed,"

explained Lulu. "Honestly, bragging about Wim Ernes admiring you. What must the other horses think?"

Blueberry sighed. He hadn't meant to sound big-headed, he had just been excited and had hoped his friends would be excited for him.

"Cheer up," said Lulu, getting to her feet and giving herself a shake. "I'm excited for you kiddo, but it's not a good idea to go around bragging about how much people think of you. It makes you sound conceited and that isn't an admirable quality. You don't hear Carl going on about what the press says about him, or how many competitions he's won, do you? After all, you didn't even know he was an Olympic rider until I told you."

Blueberry felt ashamed. Lulu was always telling him how much Carl had won, and how clever he was but Blueberry had never heard it from Carl's lips. The little brown horse's chin wobbled even more. He *had* gone on a bit. He regretted it.

"Humility," said Lulu, nodding.

"What?" asked Blueberry.

"It means being modest about your achievements and, if applicable, the compliments people give you. Best to keep quiet about it, really. Nobody likes a big-head. Plus," she added, looking very grave and serious, "you know what they say about pride, don't you?"

If Blueberry did know, then he couldn't remember. His chin wobbled some more.

"It comes before a fall," Lulu explained.

"Sorry Lulu," said Blueberry. He was. He had been a total big-head and he felt ashamed. What had he been thinking? He must have been very annoying.

"I won't tell anyone next time," he said.

"Next time?" asked Lulu, staring at him. It was amazing how searing a single eye could be when Lulu put her heart into it.

"Er, I mean, I don't suppose there will be a next time," mumbled Blueberry, totally getting it.

"Well, in the meantime, I think that it's very exciting that Wim Ernes thinks so highly of you. Now you have to live up to his expectations! You've set yourself a good old challenge there, haven't you?"

"Oh," said Blueberry, realising that everyone else he had told would probably be thinking the same thing. Maybe this keeping-quiet-humility thing was a good idea on more than one level.

Chapter Three

"**H**ave you heard the news?" asked Lulu breathlessly, worming her way into Blueberry's stable through the Lulu-sized hole she had made through the back wall for that specific purpose. Blueberry could hear the indignant clucking of the hens outside – they had scattered in all directions as Lulu had hastily galloped through them all –and he could see a white chicken feather had attached itself to Lulu's side.

20

Blueberry almost, but not quite, stopped eating his hay. It was unusual for the little tan-coloured dog to be so hyped up about anything – she always took everything in her, albeit short, stride, but something had definitely got her worked up. Blueberry lowered his head and waited for his friend to stop puffing. That she had rushed to tell him the news was obvious and he felt his heart beat faster as Lulu caught her breath. He had a feeling that whatever the news was that Lulu was going to tell him, it couldn't be good.

"It's Lydia," gasped Lulu. "She's leaving Brook Mill."

That did make Blueberry stop chewing and some soggy, half-chewed hay dropped from his mouth to his wood chippings bed below as his brain tried to make sense of what Lulu had told him. His chin worked overtime as he felt his breath catch in his throat.

"Leaving?" he repeated. "How? Why? She can't!"

"It's true," nodded Lulu, her breathing returning to normal now she had made her announcement. "I heard Carl saying how sorry he was to be losing her, and how he had to find someone special to replace her – as if he could!"

Blueberry stared out over his half-door into the distance, not noticing the immaculate stable yard, the stark silhouette of the trees in their

21

walled tubs, or the tight buds on the branches awaiting the warmth of the coming spring sunshine which would force them to burst into blossom. He didn't see the gravel drive through the archway under the grooms' quarters where Lydia lived, and The Silver Dancer piaffing on the lawn beyond.

Lydia had been his groom ever since he had arrived at Carl's dressage yard. She cared for his every need, made sure he was always comfortable. Lydia had looked after him when he had been ill. She had shed tears when he had been sent back to Holland because of his lack of height, and wept again with joy when he had returned, Carl having decided to bring him back to train as a top-class dressage horse after all. Lydia was usually the first person he saw in the morning when he woke up and looked for his breakfast, and the last person he saw at night when she checked his rugs, topped up his hay and gave him a carrot before kissing him goodnight and switching off the yard lights. Lydia couldn't leave Brook Mill. She just *couldn't*. It was unthinkable.

Blueberry felt his throat contract as he tried to control the panic he felt might overcome him. It was a mistake. Lulu was wrong. Lydia wasn't leaving – it was a joke, he told himself, a very bad, very unkind *joke*.

22

"Not funny, Lulu," Blueberry said, shaking his head so that his mane flopped on either side of his neck. "So, *soooo*, not funny!" Having decided Lulu was having a laugh at his expense, and thinking himself gullible for being taken in, Blueberry felt calmer. He wasn't going to be caught out like that!

"I would never joke about something so serious," Lulu told him gravely. "You can't possibly think I would."

The feeling of panic returned. Lulu wasn't joking. She was telling the truth. But... but... Blueberry didn't know what to do, what to think. He asked himself again and again why Lydia would leave. Had he done something wrong? Was it his fault she no longer wanted to work at Brook Mill?

"She's going to train as a veterinary nurse," Lulu explained. "You know, help vets treat us when we're ill. She'll be good at it, too. It's what she wants to do, Blueberry, so we must be happy for her and wish her good luck."

Blueberry's emotions were out of control. He remembered how Lydia had nursed him through his own illness long ago, and how she had made him feel much better. She would be a good veterinary nurse, he knew that. But he needed her to look after him. Why didn't she want to do that any more? He knew Lulu was right, that he should be happy for Lydia for pursuing a career she wanted, but instead he suddenly felt angry that she was leaving him. Who would look after him now? No one knew him as well as she did. He might not be looked after properly. Nobody knew exactly how he liked his hay – next to his water bucket so that he could dunk it in the water before chewing it. No one else knew the exact spot behind his ears where he liked to be stroked. Who else would realise how ticklish he was, and take extra care when they clipped him under his belly throughout the winter, making allowances for the way his skin shuddered and wrinkled, taking their time to ensure he was clipped smoothly?

"Are you all right?" asked Lulu.

"No," Blueberry replied. "I don't want Lydia to go. I feel like a part of me is going, too, and the future looks bleak. I can't even talk about it."

Lulu sighed. Brook Mill was unlike most equine establishments in that when people came to work there, they tended to stay. Everyone was valued, everyone had a part to play and everyone learnt so much from Carl and the horses he trained. It was rare for grooms to leave but they didn't stay forever. Lulu had been at Brook Mill for a long time, and had had to say goodbye to several people she had cared about.

For Blueberry, however, this was the first time he had lost someone close to him, someone who mattered, someone he loved.

"I'm still here, kiddo," Lulu told him, realising that with Lydia leaving, Blueberry would feel insecure and wonder about the safety of his other relationships. "Lydia is a big part of your life and you'll never forget her, but you have to let her go. You can't keep her here forever just because you want it. We all have to be happy for her and wish her well."

Blueberry gulped. He knew Lulu was right. He knew what she said made sense – he just needed some time to get his head around it all and work through his own feelings of loss.

"She will come and say goodbye to me, won't she?" he asked.

"Of course!" said Lulu. "She isn't going for a few weeks so you'll have plenty of time to say goodbye."

The little dog lay down in her favourite spot, under Blueberry's manger, keeping her one eye on her friend. He was feeling confused and upset and she would stay with him to offer support.

It was some time before Blueberry returned to his haynet and when he did so it was with a heavy heart. What would life be like at Brook Mill when Lydia left? And who would replace

25

her? Who would be his new groom? The little brown horse felt not quite complete, like someone had taken one of his legs or something. It was a weird feeling – and not very nice. He hoped it wouldn't last for ever.

The few weeks between Lulu breaking the news and Lydia leaving seemed to go faster than Blueberry could believe. He could tell his groom was excited about her new career ahead of her, and he understood she was feeling like he felt whenever he looked forward to bigger and better competitions with Charlotte and Carl, but a big part of him wanted her to stay. He hated the thought of going to competitions without her calming presence helping him, seeing to his every need. He had come to rely on her to always be there for him. He wasn't the only one who was upset – none of the horses wanted to see her go and for Willow especially, the prospect of a yard without Lydia's smiling face and easy way was almost unthinkable.

"Willow has a special soft spot for Lydia," Lulu told him, knowing how hard it was going to be for both of her friends to adjust to life without Lydia. "She's been here since he arrived, and he'll miss her more than any of us. After all," she said, "you have your career, Willow is always here, and he's always had Lydia."

Blueberry realised that Lydia wasn't just

26

there for him, but that everyone would miss her. He felt for the big mastiff-cross, Willow, who had come to Carl's from a rescue home, having been abandoned by his last owner. He could understand how he felt, how it must be even worse for him because of his history.

And although Lydia was looking forward to her new challenges, she, too, had mixed feelings about leaving all her friends.

"Will you miss me, Clyde?" she asked, offering the cat a piece of chicken from her sandwich. The ginger cat took the chicken in silence. Blueberry couldn't imagine Clyde being too bothered. Would he even notice Lydia had gone – apart from the absence of chicken pieces? Blueberry had learned that Clyde – and Bonnie, the tortoiseshell she-cat – were not exactly what you might call over-emotional. Perhaps that, he thought, feeling the ache in his heart for his soon-to-be-missed friend, wasn't such a bad thing. At least they didn't feel his heartbreak.

All too soon, it was time for Lydia to go and after a noisy party in the tack room with plenty of hugs and kisses from everyone at Brook Mill, Lydia walked around the yard saying goodbye to all the horses and cuddling the dogs. When she came to Blueberry's stable, Lydia threw her arms around his neck and shed a tear in his mane.

"Goodbye little Blueberry," she whispered. "I just know you have what it takes to go to the very top in dressage, so don't let me down. I'll always be watching to see how you progress."

Blueberry wished he could hold her coat with his teeth and make her stay but he knew he couldn't. Lulu, he noticed, was almost as upset as Willow, who followed Lydia around as if he was glued to her side, as though willing her to take him with her.

Finally, after a final look around the yard, Lydia wiped tears from her eyes, got into her car which was piled high with her things, and drove out of the gates and Blueberry's life, leaving Willow to lie down in the corner of the yard with a heavy sigh, his head on his paws, his sad eyes telling his own story. The little brown horse couldn't believe it. Lydia had gone.

Chapter Four

"This is Valegro," said Carl, "stable name Blueberry. Blueberry, meet Alan." Blueberry looked over his half-door and saw a smiling face under a baseball cap. Despite missing Lydia, the little brown horse was curious about who would look after him now she was gone, and it seemed this man, Alan, was to fill the void. The hands stroking his neck were obviously used to horses and Blueberry's heart lifted as he found the carrot Alan offered in his palm. It seemed to Blueberry that Alan had the right ideas. In the days that followed, he learned that his new personal assistant was experienced, efficient, sympathetic and very good at caring for an up-and-coming dressage horse. It appeared that Alan and Carl were old friends.

"How great that Alan's joined us!" exclaimed Lulu. She had her own reasons for liking Lydia's replacement – not that anyone thought for a second that she could be replaced, or that she was forgotten. It was just that life went on while they reserved a special place in their hearts for their absent friend. "He's helped out before and I must say, he's one of Willow's favourites. If anyone can help him get over losing Lydia, Alan can. How are you getting on, kiddo?" she asked Blueberry.

"Great," said Blueberry. "No complaints. Alan really knows what he's doing and we're getting on brilliantly." Blueberry felt pangs of guilt that he liked Alan so much. Did that mean he was being unfaithful to Lydia? He had thought he would never get over her leaving but Alan was seeing to his every need. Would Lydia be upset if he liked Alan?

"What's the matter?" asked Lulu. She had noticed a slight chin wobble. Some people wear their hearts on their sleeves. For Blueberry, his heart was firmly worn on his chin.

"I just feel a bit strange," sighed Blueberry, not really knowing how to explain it.

"Lydia won't mind, you know," said Lulu, putting her paw firmly onto Blueberry's woes. "She would want you to like Alan. Liking Alan doesn't mean you like Lydia less. It's fine to like him."

"Honestly?" asked Blueberry, feeling a huge sense of relief. How had Lulu known what he'd been thinking? She really was a wise dog. "I'm so pleased because I really do like Alan and enjoy having him around. He seems to know exactly what I need and want, even before I do. He even puts my water bucket by my haynet so I can dunk my hay in it, just like Lydia did."

"He's very experienced and he takes great pride in his work," said Lulu. And I'm pleased you're getting on because I heard Carl say that he's to go with you to your next competition. And it's a biggy – so you'll need all the help you can get."

Blueberry pricked up his ears. A big competition? What more could Lulu tell him?

"It's in the south of France, at a place called Vidauban. You don't mind the heat, do you?"

"Not at all," said Blueberry."

"And I know you don't mind travelling," added Lulu.

"I'm fine with it," Blueberry assured her.

31

"Good. It will be your first international Grand Prix, and if you and Charlotte are to be considered for Rotterdam, you'll need to achieve the qualifying score before the selectors will even notice you."

Blueberry's chin began doing its thing without him being able to control it – again! He wished it wouldn't, but there was nothing he could do about it. Lulu, of course, noticed.

"What do you mean, qualifying score?" he asked.

"Rotterdam is where the European Championships are being held this year," Lulu explained. "In Holland," she added.

Blueberry's spirits lifted. He loved going to Holland.

"So in order for the selectors to even consider you, you need to get out there and prove to them that you can do the movements required in the Grand Prix, Grand Prix Special and Grand Prix Freestyle – you know, the tests with the music."

Blueberry did. He enjoyed it when he and Charlotte did their tests to music. The tests were fun and he liked hearing the tunes, matching his strides with the notes.

"It's quite a lot to expect, a young horse like you to be noticed in his first International Grand Prix, but Carl thinks you're ready, and Charlotte is dead keen. Up for it?"

"Of course!" said Blueberry, feeling excited. If Carl thought he was ready, then ready he certainly was. This was what he wanted. He couldn't be the best dressage horse in the world if he stayed at home and didn't take chances. He was keen to compete in his first International Grand Prix so that the selectors would see him. It was his big chance!

"You've nothing to worry about," continued Lulu, noticing how keen Blueberry was. "You remember when you and Charlotte did your first Grand Prix test at Addington recently?"

Blueberry thought back to his last test at Addington, where he had been lots of times to compete. It had been an evening competition, not very big, but he had sensed it had been a big deal, he had felt the slight tension in Charlotte, letting him know that it was important to do his best. He hadn't realised they would be competing in the Grand Prix – Blueberry's first competitive Grand Prix ever. Furthermore, he hadn't realised that it was Charlotte's first Grand Prix, too.

They had practised some piaffe in the warm up but, unused to performing piaffe in the arena, Blueberry had hesitated when Charlotte asked him for the movement in the test. He had come to an uncertain halt. Was that really what she wanted him to do? But there it was,

33

the unmistakable aid, and the little brown horse had been delighted to show off his training, offering his best, highly elevated, piaffe. The hesitation had been for the merest second, barely noticeable but there all the same.

Blueberry had been overjoyed when Carl and Charlotte had started to teach him to piaffe. He knew how to do it by himself, but he hadn't been asked for the movement with anyone in his saddle until the day Charlotte asked him to trot slower and slower and slower as Carl walked beside them. And Blueberry had felt the energy fizzing up inside him more and more, as though he was storing it up – because Charlotte was not only asking him to go slower, but her legs were asking him for more impulsion, so his hind legs lifted higher and higher – and then, suddenly, he was performing the first few steps of piaffe! Charlotte and Carl had been so pleased with him – but not as pleased as Blueberry had been with himself.

As he had danced from one diagonal to the other at Addington, Blueberry's mind had flashed back to his conversation with Lulu years ago, when he had been just starting out his competitive career. She had told him then that he wouldn't be asked for the difficult movements such as piaffe and passage until he was much more experienced and competing at

34

the highest dressage levels. And there he was, performing his piaffe for Charlotte and the judges! He and Charlotte had earned a score of 75 percent that day, a score which had won them the class. It had been a memorable test for more than one reason – Blueberry had gained three maximum scores of 10 from the judges for his extended trot and his canter, and everyone had been totally over the moon. The carrots had flowed that day and Blueberry had accepted them with the graciousness of a true winner.

"If you do as well as you did at Addington," Lulu continued, briskly, bringing Blueberry back to the present with a bump, "you'll walk it and achieve your score easily. I wish I was going; it's bound to be warmer than it is here at this time of year. I can't seem to get any warmth into my bones at all lately, these March winds are bitter."

It wasn't the first time Lulu had mentioned her bones, and Blueberry was still confused about them. He couldn't understand why she wanted her bones to be warm – he saw her chewing on the odd bone now and again, growling at the other dogs if they came near her – perhaps she would prefer to chew on warm bones. Was it worth asking her about it? He decided against it.

"Will it be like it was in Spain during the

35

Sunshine Tour?" Blueberry asked. He and Charlotte had enjoyed travelling through Spain the previous year, performing with the other horses and riders on the tour. It had been fun, but they had been very serious when it had come to the dressage tests. The weather had been lovely and hot, too.

"It might be," Lulu told him, tilting her head to one side as she gave the question consideration. "But the journey shouldn't take as long. Actually, it might just be warm, rather than hot, but you never know. I understand that Vidauban is not very far from St Tropez, where all the rich and famous go for their holidays. You might bump into someone famous."

Blueberry allowed himself to wonder whether he would ever be famous enough for anyone to want to bump into him. He doubted it – but wouldn't that be ace! Apart from the bumping bit, of course, Blueberry wasn't at all sure he wanted to be bumped into if the person bumping him was large or going very fast.

The little brown horse knew when they were due to set off for Vidauban because he watched Alan loading up the horsebox with all his things the night before. In went his competition tack, followed by rugs, bandages, buckets, haynets, lots of hay and containers of water. What he wasn't aware of was all the administration that went on behind the scenes which enabled him to travel abroad and compete in international competitions.

To begin with, each horse had to have its own passport which not only proved that he was registered with the FEI, (the *Federation Equestrian International*) it also provided proof that he was a current equine member of British Dressage. In January, all the competitions Carl's horses were entered for during the coming year were submitted to British Dressage and all the international show entries were also planned. The horses were all entered for their classes, together with each horse's arrival and departure dates, passport numbers, owners' details and special requests – such as a request for a double stable for certain horses.

When the entries for each show had been confirmed, travel arrangements were organised. Shows at home were fairly straightforward but for European competitions, a ferry crossing or Channel Tunnel booking had to be made. Carl's special booking agent handled the crossings and ensured all the necessary health papers were in order. If the papers weren't completed perfectly then the horse could be stopped at the port and sent back home. The Channel Tunnel was Carl's preferred choice, as ferry crossings could be rough in bad weather and the ferry companies could refuse to take the horsebox. Just like people, horses can suffer from seasickness – only it can be worse for horses because they can't actually be sick. Their throats are designed to allow food only one way – from throat to stomach – not the other way around.

But that's not all. For travelling abroad, the vet has to check each horse's travel papers before they leave the yard to ensure they are in order. A health certificate for each horse has to be applied for through Defra (The Department of Environment, Food and Rural Affairs). Plus, each horse needs an export licence before they can leave and return home.

Even when the horses do arrive home there is paperwork to see to, which is all collected and filed in case Defra wants to inspect the export licence. These can be requested at any time during the six months following a horse's journey to check they are in order. Carl's office is full of bulging filing cabinets! Getting horses to international competitions is more complicated than just entering a show and getting there! Luckily, the logistics of international journeys was of no concern to Blueberry. He knew that the pyramid of people under him, Carl and Charlotte, was crowded, but it was more crowded than he could ever have imagined.

With all the terrifying and exhaustive paperwork in order, and Blueberry's luggage packed and loaded, he was able to leave Brook Mill with Alan at the wheel of the air-conditioned horsebox the next day. The journey went well, and the horsebox made good progress down to the south of France to Vidauban. But when they arrived and the ramp was lowered, Blueberry looked out on what he thought was going to be a sunny day and got a shock. Heavy black clouds hid any sunshine that was trying to get through. It had been a brighter day back at Brook Mill!

'Well,' thought Blueberry, as Alan made sure he was comfortable in his stable accommodation, 'I don't think Lulu would be very impressed with this weather. No chance of warm bones here!'

He was glad to see Carl and Charlotte when they arrived and Blueberry couldn't wait to get into the arena and show everyone what he could do. Perhaps the sun would shine tomorrow. He hoped so.

It didn't. The next day dawned just as black overhead and as Blueberry and Charlotte warmed up and worked in prior to their test, big splats of rain began to fall, making everyone wish the competition was indoors. No such luck – it was a big outdoor arena, with nowhere to escape the weather.

Blueberry clamped his tail down to prevent

the rain from dripping down inside his hind legs, and hunched his back. At least the rain wasn't as cold as at home, but it still made things difficult. The track beneath his hooves felt no different and there was no danger of him slipping but trying to perform dressage movements in the rain wasn't as enjoyable as it would have been in the sunshine everyone had anticipated.

The clock ticked on and the weather didn't improve. It wasn't long before Blueberry and Charlotte were due to ride their test and the weather showed no sign of getting any better. If anything, the rain was coming down even harder.

"What do you want to do?" asked Carl, hunching his shoulders against the rain which was pouring down and soaking everyone. It truly was terrible weather. "Do you want to withdraw?"

Blueberry held his breath. They had come all this way. The selectors wouldn't even see them if they didn't go ahead with the competition.

Charlotte shook her head. She and Blueberry had come to Vidauban to achieve a qualifying score for the up-and-coming European Championships. If they withdrew, any chance they might have to be selected would be lost. As she turned Blueberry towards the entrance to the arena, Blueberry let out a huge sigh of relief.

They were going for it! But it wouldn't be easy, not in the torrential rain when all he wanted to do was stick his head down and huddle up against the wet. But he had to do his best – it was just for a few minutes. He could do it!

As soon as they entered the arena Blueberry knew he wouldn't allow the rain to beat him, to rob him of his chance to impress the selectors. He drew himself up and ignored the raindrops falling into his ears. He forgot the water dripping down his face and into his eyes and nostrils. He lifted his tail as his back began to work, ignoring the water running down his hind legs and soaking his hocks. His hooves squelched on the arena surface but Blueberry concentrated totally on his rider. He was Valegro, the dressage horse, competing at Grand Prix, and he was here to prove to everyone just how good he was.

Of course, there were not as many people there to see him as he had hoped, and those that had stayed were huddled under umbrellas, but Blueberry knew he only had to perform for the judges watching him from the dry of their little sheds, hoping to be impressed. Impress them he would!

It wasn't just the rain Vidauban was remembered for that year; it was the fact that a little brown horse from England, Valegro, together with his equally unknown rider, won both their Grands Prix and the Grand Prix Special at their first international Grand Prix competition. The young, green horse on his international debut performed virtually mistake-free tests in the rain with his equally un-tested rider, causing the dressage world to sit up and take notice. If only a few people knew who Valegro was before Vidauban, *everybody* was talking about him afterwards. Blueberry had made an impression, one which no one who watched him at Vidauban would ever forget.

Chapter Five

Saumur, in western France, was Blueberry and Uti's next venue. Saumur is where the French National Riding School has its base. The French military mounted display team, the Cadre Noir, which travels the world thrilling audiences old and new, is based at the riding school, and the instructors train the horses and teach riders to ride in the classical manner.

Blueberry and Uthopia were destined to compete with Charlotte and Carl in their saddles respectively. Ten-year-old Uti was familiar with the venue as he and Carl had won there the previous year, and to everyone's delight they once more took first place in the Grand Prix. The remarkable thing was that Blueberry, a whole year younger than Uti, came second to his stable mate with a score only a single percentage point below. Even more remarkably, the placings were reversed in the Grand Prix Special, with Blueberry taking top place and Uti a mere sniff behind him.

Blueberry could hardly believe it when Charlotte guided him to stand above his friend in the prize-giving. Was it possible they had achieved a higher score than Uti and Carl? Nervously, Blueberry looked sideways at his travelling companion to see whether he was upset or annoyed with him and at first it seemed his worries were founded.

"Who said you could beat me?" asked Uti, sternly. Blueberry gulped, his eyes wide. "Don't look so upset," his friend continued, "I'm only joking! You and Charlotte did a beautiful test – if I'm going to lose to anyone, I'm delighted it's you."

"Really?" said Blueberry, hugely relieved.

"Of course," said Uti. "We're on the same team, remember!"

Blueberry hadn't thought of it like that. Of

course, it wasn't just about the team of himself, Charlotte and Carl, it was about Team Brook Mill, and he and Uti were on the same side. What really mattered was that Team Brook Mill was successful.

In the same spirit, Carl was delighted with everyone's performances and gratified that his plan to campaign Blueberry and Charlotte for London 2012 seemed to be working. Just as he had planned, their next stop would be the European Championships in Rotterdam in August that year!

Every two weeks someone very special came to Brook Mill. Of all the horses on Carl's yard it was Blueberry who looked forward to this visitor the most. Besides eating and dressage, his fortnightly sessions with Marnie, the equine sports physiotherapist, were his favourite thing to do.

Their sessions took place in Blueberry's stable, where it was quiet, and Marnie would stand on a stool to reach the top of the little brown horse's back. She had what Blueberry liked to call 'magic hands', rubbing them all over his body, finding any muscles which were tight and working them in a special way until they felt good again. Marnie's hands worked all around Blueberry's body, pulling, pushing and banging in a way that made his whole being feel massaged and pampered, relaxed yet energised at the same time.

Blueberry found Marnie's sessions so relaxing, he often dozed off as she worked. Strangely, though, her work sometimes made him feel thirsty and when that happened he would tug at his headcollar rope to make it clear he needed a drink – which Marnie was happy to supply.

Equine physiotherapists are highly trained. They need to qualify as human physiotherapists before training further for their veterinary physiotherapy degree, and then undertake even more exams if they wish to specialise in horse therapy. And being one of the best, Marnie had some pretty high-class sporting equine customers on her books. All the horses at Carl's yard enjoyed their sessions with Marnie. Just like humans, equine athletes can sometimes suffer twinges and muscular strains. Dressage, although asking for only natural movements a horse would perform without a rider, is still hard work. Just as human dancers and gymnasts need to look after their bodies and ensure they are fit, so do equine ones. The movements look graceful but they are physically demanding, and require a great deal of effort.

Having regular sessions with a physio means

46

any small problems can be identified before they graduate to big problems, and keeping muscles in the peak of condition can only help horses enjoy their work. If a muscle is painful then it will influence how a horse moves – he may move differently to save that muscle, setting up a chain of problems which will be harder, if not impossible to cure. For dressage horses, just as with all equine athletes working at the top of their game, using their bodies in the most efficient way, without stress on muscles and joints, is imperative for maximum performance. Nobody can give a top performance if something hurts, or niggles, or causes them to move differently to how they should.

After Marnie's sessions Blueberry was always relaxed and sleepy. But one day, no sooner had he been rugged up again and was watching her car disappear down the driveway towards the gates to the road, another car drove in. It was the car every horse on the yard looked forward to seeing the *least*.

"That's not… *you know who*, is it?" asked Orange, lifting his head high like a giraffe, his ears brushing the top of his door frame, his eyes like saucers.

"Oh no," said Blueberry, turning around in his stable and facing the back wall in denial.

The car everyone recognised belonged to the vet.

"I know he means well," said Uti, who had noticed the car's arrival, too, "but every visit means us either trotting up and down the yard for his perusal, or having a light shone into our eyes or our hearts listened to, or some other test being exerted upon us."

"Don't forget the jabs," Orange reminded him. Unsurprisingly, needles were high on his list of things not to like.

"Oh thanks," said Blueberry, still facing the wall, "the jabs were the thing I was most hoping to forget!"

"You lot ought to be grateful that the vet takes so much care about your health," scolded Lulu, who had trotted onto the yard and seen the reaction of its occupants. "Carl is only making sure you are all in tip-top condition and as healthy as can be. Look at me, where would I be without the skill and care of the vet who removed my eye to save my life? And if you'd ever seen how some poor horses are neglected, you'd welcome the vet's arrival."

Blueberry felt ashamed. "Sorry, Lulu," he said. He realised how strongly his friend felt about the vet by the very fact she had mentioned the loss of her eye – it was something about which she had never spoken before.

"Those vaccination jabs prevent you from catching horrible, incurable diseases," Lulu continued, still cross. "And if you don't have them, and Carl can't produce the papers to prove it, none of you would be able to go to any shows, let alone travel and compete abroad."

Whereas Orange thought that could only be a good thing, Blueberry didn't like the sound of it at all! Which was why, when Alan held his headcollar and the vet produced a syringe and gave Blueberry his injection, he stood as still as a rock, then took an interest when he signed some paperwork before handing it to his groom. There was no way he was going to hamper any procedures necessary for him to compete in dressage – either home or away. Bring it on, he thought. The vet could stick as many needles into him as he liked, until he looked like a hedgehog, just as long as it meant he could compete.

Chapter Six

"Here we are then, Blueberry," said Alan, leading the little brown horse down the ramp of the horsebox and to his stable at the European Championships in Rotterdam's Kralingse Bos Park. As he walked along the path, Blueberry took in all the stables filled with horses from all over Europe. Top dressage horses, the best their countries had to send, were all there. Their grooms were busy cleaning tack, filling water buckets, grooming their charges and chatting to each other. Blueberry's stable was between his friend Uthopia and a tall chestnut with a long white blaze down his face, Laura Bechtolsheimer's Mistral Højris, known by his stable name, Alf, also on the British Dressage Team. Blueberry had met Alf before at competitions, and knew him to be one of the top dressage horses in the country. He was thrilled to be in a team with them both.

"I always enjoy coming home," said Uthopia said between mouthfuls of hay, "don't you?"

Blueberry agreed. Not only did he enjoy being back in Holland, with the familiar sound of the language all around him, but Blueberry appreciated that the journey to Rotterdam from Brook Mill was a short one. He never minded travelling, but long journeys could be tiring.

"This is a very big competition," Uthopia told Blueberry, sending a shiver along his team mate's spine. The little brown horse wasn't nervous, he was excited. Hadn't he always dreamed of competing at the very big competitions? He had made it. How he performed here would dictate whether he was destined to be selected for further international teams. He had Charlotte and Carl who believed in him, but here was his chance to prove to everyone else that he was worthy of his place on the team.

A huge grey horse was led past the stables by a groom, followed by an equally large bay. Blueberry felt the very first twinges of doubt in his mind. How could he feel so confident one moment, and filled with apprehension and doubt the next? Could he, the little brown horse from England, really hold his own against the big, experienced horses of Europe? He wished Lulu had been able to come with them. She always knew exactly how to put any doubts he might have aside. What would she say to him, he wondered, his mind drifting back to Brook Mill.

As he daydreamed he saw not the competition stables at Rotterdam, but the yard he loved so much at home. He could hear the hens clucking as they scratched at the gravel, see Bonnie and Clyde sitting in the tree, looking down on him in the superior way only cats can. He heard the bustle of the grooms in the tack room, sweeping the yard, filling the haynets. And there was Lulu, scratching behind one ear with her hind leg, telling him that he only had to do what he did at home, just do his best, that it would be good enough and that he had Carl and Charlotte with him and they were a formidable team. He heard her reminding him of his dream, his dream which had carried him this far, got him through his doubts, kept him going, his dream to be the best dressage horse in the world.

The image faded in his mind and Blueberry was back at Rotterdam. He was Blueberry –

Valegro – and here was his opportunity to realise his dream, and he wasn't going to waste it by doubting himself.

Team GB were not the favourites to win in Rotterdam. The British had never won any gold medals in international dressage competitions, having always had to watch the mighty Germans and Dutch sweep the board, and dream of what might be. Besides that, Uthopia and Blueberry were inexperienced horses at international level, how could they possibly be in with a shout of finishing in the medals so early in their careers? Blueberry could feel how the horses on the other teams felt about him and his team mates. The other horses were confident; they were here to win – they *expected* to win. As he and Charlotte rode around in the warm up arena on the day before the competition, he couldn't miss the way the bigger horses looked at him in surprise, and he overheard their comments – the nature with which he was familiar.

"Who's zee poneee?"

"The British, zay have only zee tiny horses to ride, eh?"

"This one, he needs to grow a bit before he can be on a team, no?"

"How can a 'orse with such leetle legs do zee tempi-changes, I wonder."

"The British have so few good horses, they are bringing their babies with them now!"

"Are you lost, maybe? The pony championships are not 'ere, not now, ha ha!"

Blueberry's ears rang with all the comments. He didn't know what to say. He remembered Lulu's talk about humility but, even so, he longed to tell all the rude horses that they would soon be eating their words and that he, Valegro, would be a name they would remember long after these championships were over. But he didn't dare. What if they were right? What if the judges agreed with them and thought he was too small? How could he make them change their minds? What must he do to convince them that he was worthy of their attention?

Not all the horses were so unkind. One or two told him to take no notice of the negative comments.

"They try to mess with your brain," said one elegant brown mare, who seemed to float on air whenever Blueberry saw her perform the tempi-changes at every stride for her rider as they exercised. "They should concentrate on their own performances. Everyone knows you should never underestimate zee competition. That way, they set themselves up for a shock, no?"

Blueberry was grateful for the support – it

seemed to be in short supply. Of course, Uti and Alf told him to take no notice of the other horses, too.

"Don't waste your time worrying about their opinion," snorted Alf. "Just do your best, that's all Carl and Charlotte ask."

Blueberry was grateful for the support but, even so, the unkind words haunted his dreams at night, and he found it difficult to put them out of his mind. They were in there, he couldn't turn back time and un-hear them. Once again he wished Lulu was with him to give him confidence. But then, Blueberry thought, he had to learn to cope with setbacks himself, he couldn't always rely on Lulu. She couldn't travel with him abroad. Even so, just thinking about his friend helped and he knew *she* would never let the opinions of others upset her.

Feeling better, Blueberry slept well, practising all his favourite dressage movements in his sleep, his legs twitching as his dreams were filled with canter pirouettes, one and two-time changes and zig-zag half-passes across the arena.

In the morning, Blueberry awoke feeling full of confidence. Of course, he thought, actions speak louder than words – he had heard Lulu say that. Let the other horses think he was too small, that he was no danger to them. Let them underestimate him. Blueberry made up his mind to show them all. He would try his hardest and hope it would be enough to prove how wrong they were to judge him simply on how he looked.

'A dressage horse is judged on how well he dances,' thought Blueberry. 'So I'll dance like no dressage horse has ever danced before. I won't let Charlotte and Carl down – or you, Lulu. You've always believed in me, and I'm going to repay your faith. I'm going to do the very best test I've ever done – or burst trying!'

Chapter Seven

It was time for the Grand Prix. As Blueberry stood waiting for Charlotte to tell him when to enter the arena, his mind wandered back to Uthopia's recent return to the stable area after his Grand Prix performance with Carl.

"How did you do?" Blueberry had asked him – although seeing everyone's reactions left him in no doubt that his friend had done something incredible.

"It was amazing," Uti told him as his saddle was taken off. "I don't know what happened but something suddenly clicked in my head and I felt as though I was floating on air. My test was so light, so effortless. I've never felt like that in a test and I know Carl was overcome. Every judge gave me a score of 10 for my extended trot across the diagonal – every one! I still feel like I'm on cloud nine and my final score was over 82 percent. It was just magical."

Blueberry had been thrilled for his friend, and his success had given the whole team a boost. Suddenly, they had a chance of finishing in the medals! Laura and Mistral Højris performed beautifully and achieved a great score of 77 percent, which meant that the two combined scores put Team GB in a medal-winning position with their last horse to go. The final result rested on Blueberry and Charlotte. Could it be possible that they could rise to the occasion, or would the pressure prove too much for such an inexperienced pair? Could their performance win Team GB a medal?

Blueberry could feel the atmosphere in the air. The whole arena was electric. The Dutch Team were in silver medal position with Germany – predictably – in gold. Could the little brown horse and his inexperienced rider really cause an upset to the status quo? Was it too much to ask? Would nerves prove the superior comments of the other horses to be true?

Trotting around the dressage boards, awaiting their turn, Blueberry remembered those comments but instead of feeling intimidated, he drew strength from them. Those horses had dismissed him as being no threat to them. They had already decided the little horse was no competition. Blueberry felt his heart swell – now it was time to put all his training into practice. Now was the time to show everyone his ambition, his determination. He had to concentrate. As Charlotte asked him to turn and ride inside the white markers, Blueberry arched his neck. He hadn't come all this way just to make up the numbers. He was here to carry out his plan, his dream, to dance like no other horse had ever danced, to prove that Carl's faith in him hadn't been misplaced.

Blueberry danced. But no – he and Charlotte didn't just dance, they danced with flair, they danced with joy, they danced with passion. When Blueberry had executed his passage, his half passes, his canter pirouettes, his piaffe and his beautiful tempi-changes, when he had come to a halt at the end of his test and stood, four-square and felt Charlotte drop his reins and hug his neck the little brown horse felt as though he was eighteen hands high. He had done his best and he couldn't have done any better. Was it enough?

The crowd went wild. Just as they had after Uti's test, they took to their feet and cheered and cheered. Not only could they appreciate the beauty of the test they had just seen, but the home crowd loved the fact that the two horses, Uthopia and Valegro, were Dutch-bred, and nationalistic pride was generously extended to the pair from the British team.

Walking out of the arena, Blueberry and Charlotte met up with their mentor and trainer.

"I've been in pieces watching you two," said Carl, with tears in his eyes. "I could barely watch – luckily I found a pillar to hide behind and peek around. You were both amazing. Well done!"

Blueberry's heart swelled again – this time with pride. He had so wanted to make Carl proud of him and it seemed his trainer was certainly delighted.

Blueberry and Charlotte's performance made British dressage history that day. Their mark of 78 per cent put Team GB into the team gold medal position for the Grand Prix, the highest placing a British dressage team had ever achieved, and the highest ever international dressage score for Britain, too. It was an amazing achievement and a moment

60

no-one connected with British dressage will ever forget. For a young, inexperienced horse and an equally inexperienced rider to be part of the first British gold-medal-winning team at a European Championships was nothing short of miraculous.

Standing with an emotional Alan behind the podium, flanked by Uti and Alf, Blueberry felt he had achieved all he had set out to do – and more. He was the little brown horse from Team GB, but the little brown horse to be reckoned with. Never again would the other horses underestimate him. He had proved his worth.

Chapter Eight

Pride comes before a fall, Lulu had said. Blueberry had cause to remember his friend's words later in the Championships.

After a relaxed day off following the Team Grand Prix competition, the top placed horses and riders prepared themselves for the individual Grand Prix Special. The horses and riders who finished in the top fifteen in this competition would qualify for the Freestyle, ridden to music, test. The results of both competitions would decide the final individual placings. Carl and Charlotte had both qualified for the Grand Prix Special, but the timings of their tests meant that Carl was busy with Uti and concentrating on his own test, when normally he would have been helping Charlotte in her preparation. As a result, Blueberry felt the tiny tremors of indecision in his rider as they warmed up.

Every rider benefits from having their trainer present to help them before a competition and because they were both at the start of their international careers, Charlotte and Blueberry felt a little lost without Carl offering his valued encouragement and advice. It wasn't as though they needed constant instruction but something was missing, and their usual routine suffered from this hiccup. The psychology of riding is something team trainers have recognised for years, and great emphasis is placed on psychological training for all riders. Just a momentary negative thought can have a devastating effect of a rider's performance and confidence. Positive thinking is everything. Even though it isn't something available to horses, even the most miniscule hesitation or indecision on the part of a rider is felt by their mount, such is the bond of each partnership.

All through each test the pair tried their

hardest, and Blueberry could feel that he had executed some fantastic movements, but others hadn't felt quite how he would have wanted. There was a hesitation here, a lost transition there – even a missed tempi-change. During the Freestyle, also known as the Kur, a couple of music cues were fluffed, and Blueberry had come out of both tests disappointed with himself. They had already won a team gold medal, they had nothing to prove, and yet he felt he could have done more, and he knew Charlotte felt the same about herself. Carl and Uti carried the flag for them, however, winning a silver medal in both classes, and Blueberry was delighted for his friend.

"We've both done well," Uti said, when Blueberry congratulated him back at the stables. "You mustn't be downhearted about your tests – we're not machines, and neither are our riders. It's tough for us to be at the top of our game in every single test."

Blueberry knew Uti was right – didn't Carl tell them the very same thing whenever they had an off-day? It was unrealistic to expect perfect performances every time. But Blueberry was his own fiercest critic and he felt he could have, *should* have, done better. He vowed he would work harder. He hadn't enjoyed the disappointment he had felt coming out of the arena after his less-than-brilliant tests. He didn't want to feel like that again. The feeling he craved was the one he remembered when he had watched Carl and Charlotte mount the podium to collect their medals. He had been proud, and he had loved the way the crowd had responded after his gold-medal-winning test, cheering and waving, on their feet and clapping. He had felt their appreciation, and couldn't wait to experience it again.

"I can't wait to tell everyone at home about our gold medals!" exclaimed Uti. "Won't they be amazed?"

Blueberry couldn't either. He would tell them modestly, he decided, but even so it was difficult to keep the excitement out of his voice when he told his friends Orange and Lulu all about his adventures in Holland. What a contrast to his trip back to his homeland when he had been a youngster, before Carl had decided to keep him and train him on. Then he had been upset and depressed. Now, memories of Holland were happy and successful, and demons had been laid to rest.

"All your dreams are coming true, kiddo," said Lulu, when Orange had retreated back into his stable to munch on his hay, and the stables were quiet save for the odd hoot of an owl and a bark of a fox in the darkness.

"They are, Lulu, they are," sighed Blueberry. "I'm the luckiest horse alive. I have been given the opportunity to train with one of the best dressage trainers in the world, and have one of the best riders to help me. At this moment, I don't think I will ever be happier than I am now. I'm a European gold medal winning dressage horse. I can hardly believe it!"

"I'm happy for you, you've worked really hard for it," said his friend. "And how was Alan?"

"Oh, he's great," said Blueberry. "He not only looks after me but he's very protective, too. With Alan with me I know nothing bad will ever happen to me, and I can relax at competitions and on my journeys knowing he will make sure I have everything I need and want. Oh, and he's handy with the apples and carrots, too, so he's totally ace in my book!"

Lulu snorted – then she was off on one of her moonlit sniff-a-thons, seeking out wild scents and following trails Blueberry couldn't see, enjoying the heady scents of the night, hoping to come across something small and furry to chase. Blueberry watched her criss-cross her way along the grass in the silvery light, passing The Silver Dancer still and serene as always on the lawn, the ever-changing red, green and amber lights bouncing off the metal back, highlighting the hooves held forever in the perfect piaffe.

"There were moments in Rotterdam when I was like The Silver Dancer," murmured Blueberry, re-living his finest moment, sighing as the memories flooded back. He would experience that feeling again, he was determined to.

Chapter Nine

"**I**t's that time of year again, isn't it?" asked Blueberry. The grooms had hung up what looked like long, fat, fluffy cats' tails all around the yard and on the horses' stable doors, only these tails sparkled in the lights and twinkled in the moonlight. "What's it called again?"

"Christmas," said Lulu. "It's bonkers."

"That's it," murmured Blueberry, "*Christmas*. I remember it from last year. Everyone laughed a lot and the grooms sang songs late one evening. I remember there were a lot of bangs and pops going on in their rooms over the stables, which kept us all awake one night."

"Hmmm," snorted Lulu, disapproving of the grooms' Christmas party, mainly because she had been banking on there being some left-over sausage rolls and chipolatas-on-sticks, but every single one of them had been eaten, along with the turkey sandwiches. Furthermore, there had been plenty of sore heads on the yard the morning after and more than one or two grumpy people to avoid. It seemed to Lulu that Christmas had a lot to answer for.

"Well the party won't get under way until after Olympia," Lulu continued. "You'll be going there this year. You'll love it. I might even sneak along myself. There's usually a cake or two to be had in the horsebox when nobody's looking."

"What's Olympia?" asked Blueberry.

"It's a show, a big show in London. Dressage is on the agenda for the first two days, and then the show jumpers take over for the rest of the week, with lots of displays for the audience. It has a party atmosphere, everyone loves it, and there's even classes for dogs – although all that running around and jumping over things, going through tunnels and wriggling between poles is not something I'd get too excited about. A dog can waste a lot of energy wriggling through poles. I mean, what's wrong with travelling in a straight line?"

Blueberry hadn't a clue what Lulu was talking about. Poles? Tunnels? The only tunnel he knew was the Channel Tunnel – he'd been through it several times on his way to shows on the Continent. He hadn't been asked to wriggle between any poles, though. He wondered how that would feel. A bit like doing his canter half-passes in zig-zag, probably.

"What are show jumpers?" he asked.

"Horses that jump over things for a living. Huge great jumps made up of poles, bushes, water and walls. I mean really huge – some jumps are as high as Carl."

More poles, thought Blueberry. Olympia seemed to be a bit pole-obsessed.

"I won't be asked to jump, will I?" he asked.

"No. Fancy it, do you?"

Blueberry thought it might be fun but it sounded like hard work. Could some horses really jump as high as Carl? He didn't think he could do that. Why, that was higher than the fence around the field! He'd stick to dressage.

"You'll be going on the two dressage days – of course," Lulu reassured him. "The Grand Prix and Grand Prix Freestyle there are qualifiers for something called the World Cup. The World Cup final will be held somewhere else at the end of the season in spring, but to be in it horses have to qualify and Olympia offers an opportunity to do just that. Everyone wants to win a World Cup qualifier so they can go on to have a crack at winning the World Cup itself. It means you've won lots of competitions throughout the season, and have won against all the top horses in the world."

Blueberry couldn't help thinking that there were a lot of competitions he still didn't know about. Would winning the World Cup be an ambition too far for him, he wondered. It sounded daunting – yet wonderful at the same time.

"Will there many people be watching at Olympia?" he asked.

"Loads. It's not a good place if you're shy and retiring – like our ginger chum," Lulu whispered, nodding towards Orange's stable. "The arena is surrounded by seating and the people watching are all above you at ear-height. It's pretty awesome, actually. Why don't you ask Uti about it?"

So Blueberry did, and Uti was just as enthusiastic.

"Great show – and it's indoors of course, so there's no rain or wind to worry about. The audience really gets behind the horses, they're enthusiasts. You'll love it, I know how much you love an audience!"

71

Blueberry couldn't wait. As it happened, he didn't have to as Alan began loading the horsebox that very afternoon and Blueberry was washed and groomed the following morning, loaded beside Uti, and the pair set off for London.

"We're nearly there," Uti told him, as the horsebox slowed down to negotiate the heavy city traffic. Blueberry could hear the cars, vans and taxis all around him, see flyovers and bridges through the windows and smell the heavy, smoky atmosphere of the capital city. London didn't smell very nice, not at all like the clear, clean air of Gloucestershire. He hoped Olympia wasn't going to be as bad as the London roads.

The Grand Hall at Olympia is right in the heart of London, and space is tight. Blueberry and Uti were unloaded in a tiny concrete area and led to temporary stables behind the main arena. Lots of other dressage horses were already there, and Blueberry could see them exercising in a crowded arena by the stables, all the riders being extra careful not to bump into each other. The main arena was also available for exercise – but only at certain times of the day – and Blueberry saw his first sight of the big indoor arena the following morning, together with the other horses.

Lulu had been right, huge banks of red seating

72

rose up around the arena on all sides, topped by private boxes where people would sit eating and drinking during the forthcoming days. It would have felt very claustrophobic if it hadn't been for the beautiful glass ceiling high, high above Blueberry's head, through which natural light flooded. He and Uti, with Charlotte and Carl aboard, stretched their legs before being asked for a few dressage movements and as they reached the far side of the arena and turned around to face the entrance, Blueberry was astonished to see statues of three huge golden horses rearing up above the black curtains which separated the outside practise arena from the main one. Whereas Carl had The Silver Dancer at home, it appeared that Olympia had its own trio of golden horses leaping towards the arena.

'How amazing to be immortalised in gold,' thought Blueberry. He thought The Silver Dancer was pretty cool, but the huge golden horses were certainly impressive.

The whole hall had been decorated in tinsel, and there were huge advertising boards below the seats, which Blueberry found a bit off-putting to start with. He had seen similar boards at other competitions but these seemed closer and larger. He was glad they were able to practise in the main arena so he could get used to it all – he would have found it difficult to concentrate if he'd been asked to perform his test without knowing all this beforehand.

Blueberry recognised Mistral Højris, aka Alf, with Laura in the saddle, as well as some of the other horses he had competed against in Rotterdam. It was Christmas, it was festive in the hall and there was definitely a special atmosphere about the place but everyone was concentrating hard on their work, just as they did at all the other shows throughout the year. Blueberry put his head down and listened to Charlotte. He would do his best here, at Olympia, just as he did everywhere else.

Chapter Ten

Something strange happened after Olympia that Blueberry never fully understood – and he wasn't the only one. The day after they returned home, Uti came out of his stable in the morning, limping.

"It's my foot," he told Blueberry, after Carl, the grooms and the vet had all examined him. "I don't know why, but it just hurts. I think I overdid it in my tests at Olympia. I should know better, really, but I wanted to do well. I just suffer from sensitive feet – you're so lucky having strong, cobby hooves."

"Poor you," said Blueberry, in sympathy, and wondering whether he ought to be upset by Uti's remarks about his own hooves. It seemed like he'd been given a compliment, but then it also seemed like Uti had been quite rude about his feet, too. Instead of going out in the field next to Blueberry and Orange, Uti had to remain in his stable.

"You boys can be a bit rough out here," said Alan, as he closed the field gate behind Blueberry and watched him gallop off before rearing up to play with Orange. "And that's just what Uti doesn't need!" he added, before returning to the yard.

"Tell me again about Olympia." said Orange, as they settled down to graze. The grass was never very tasty in December, and the horses always had to wait until any frost had melted before they were turned out, but it was better than nothing. They would get all their nutrients from their hay and feed, but eating grass gave them the chance to chill out and relax, and putting their heads down stretched their toplines – which helped them in their work. Strong muscles had built up along the top of their necks and backs due to their dressage training, and keeping those muscles in good order was essential.

"The huge crowd watching me was seated above my ears – all around me," began Blueberry, excitement filling his mind as he thought back to Olympia. "In the evening the glass roof was dark because of the night sky. I would have liked to have been able to stare up at it to see whether I could spot the stars through it, but I was too busy."

"The roof sounds nice," said Orange, carefully sorting a twig from the grass with his tongue and casting it aside, "but the crowd sounds a nightmare. How could you concentrate?"

"I had to," replied Blueberry. "Besides, I find I perform better when I have a crowd watching. I don't know why, it's just part of the whole performance. I feel lifted. Without the crowd I might as well be at home or just practising."

A shiver went through Orange, but Blueberry knew he liked to hear about his travels. There was something oddly fascinating about hearing stories of scenarios Orange dreaded which made him compelled to listen to his friend. Blueberry had noticed that the bright chestnut horse was going to fewer and fewer competitions these days, and working mainly at home with Carl's pupils who were learning a great deal from riding such a good horse. Orange was happier training the students, but Blueberry wondered whether he would ever go to a competition again. Surely Carl would have preferred him to compete?

"Before going into the arena we all had to warm up backstage," Blueberry continued, "and soon it was time for me and Charlotte to do our test. We had to go into a tunnel – between backstage and the main arena – and wait. They had these enormous black curtains across the tunnel so you couldn't see the arena and they were drawn back when it was our turn. I could see the dressage markers all laid out, and as we walked into the light a murmur rippled throughout the audience as the commentator announced who we were."

"Go on," said Orange, rubbing his nose on a front leg.

"I could feel how important the competition was – Charlotte seemed very serious – so I knew I had to concentrate. When we began our test, the crowd were completely silent and I almost forgot they were there. You know how it is, you get lost in the moment and it's as though you're in a bubble, just you and your rider."

Orange had never felt like that at a competition which was why he always found it so difficult to concentrate. He didn't say so because Blueberry was in full flow, remembering Olympia.

"Our Grand Prix test was good – I could feel it. Everything seemed to go right and at the end

78

Charlotte was pretty thrilled. The crowd went wild when we finished, which was lovely. As we walked out of the arena I looked up and around, as if to thank everyone for their support – and Charlotte waved. It was so great!"

"Did the judges think so?" asked Orange.

"They did, because our mark was over 81 percent – and I heard Carl say we were the only ones in the competition with a score over 80! And, when we came back into the arena again later, we stood in first place under the spotlights. I was so proud! Carl and Roly – you know, my other owner – were there, and Alan, and everyone was so happy. Charlotte and I led all the other riders and horses around the arena, then we completed a lap of honour by ourselves, with everyone clapping." Blueberry sighed at the memory.

"Well done!" said Orange, meaning it. He was always glad for his friend's success.

"But that wasn't all," continued Blueberry. "We competed in the Grand Prix Freestyle, to music, and although we didn't win we did come second to Laura and Alf. Carl and Uti were third. And you'll never guess what our marks were."

"Er, 81 again?" suggested Orange.

"Even better. Uti, Alf and I *all* got marks over 83! Alf got the highest mark of all of us. I was

79

more excited in the Grand Prix Freestyle and a bit nervous to start with. I could have kicked myself because I fluffed the tempi-changes and was feeling pretty awful about it but Charlotte was right on it because she asked me to do them in a different part of the test. I wondered what she was doing at first because I knew they weren't supposed to be there, but I did as she asked and realised she had put them in to show the judges I really could do them – and that time I did them perfectly. It was such a special prize-giving, everyone seemed quite emotional. I think someone said it was the first time a British rider had won the World Cup Qualifier there – that was Laura and Alf – and I was the youngest horse in the class. Someone called Stephen Clarke said our performances were… hold on, let me get this right, I heard Carl say it a couple of times… *A dream come true from a national point of view.*"

"What does that mean?" asked Orange.

"I think it means that Uti, Alf and I are doing well for Team GB – or perhaps it means we might be able to do well in the future. Do you think it will help us get selected for the Olympics?"

"It might," said Orange, not really understanding what Blueberry was talking about, but wanting to be supportive. "Who's Stephen Clarke?"

"He's a very important person in British Dressage, apparently," said Blueberry, and as he said it he remembered what Lulu had told him about humility. "You don't think I'm being big-headed telling you this, do you?" he asked. He didn't feel as though he was boasting, he was just telling Orange how things had been.

"Of course not," Orange reassured him. He was interested in hearing how his friend had performed, and happy he was achieving his dream. "Tell me some more, I like hearing about it – it's much better than having to go there myself."

The little brown horse continued his account of his time at the big Christmas show, telling Orange about the hugs and tears after the prize-giving, how Alan had got him ready for his journey home through the dark and quiet of London in the early hours of the morning, and how he had been too excited to sleep. Eventually, the sun started to go down and Alan and one of the other grooms came to fetch them in.

"How are you feeling, Uti?" Blueberry asked as soon as his rugs were changed and he had started on his haynet. He always thought hay tasted quite dry, which was why he liked to dunk each mouthful in his water bucket before chewing. Dry hay made him thirsty so his method of soaking it kept him feeling refreshed.

"A bit better, but my foot is still sore," Uti replied, sounding a bit sorry for himself.

Blueberry chewed his hay with relish. Not only did he love the taste of his soggy hay but, Lulu had explained, eating and digesting an almost constant supply of the dried grass helped to keep him warm. Hay, Lulu had said, was central heating for horses. And no, she had added, lifting a paw at Blueberry suggestion, she wouldn't like to try it, thanks. Hay didn't feature on Lulu's list of tasty treats but she did suggest that if Blueberry was ever offered a dog biscuit, she'd appreciate him passing it on to her. As if that was likely to happen, Blueberry had thought.

As night drew in, the cockerel and his hens took themselves off to the safety of their chicken coop and the cats sloped off to the warmth of the hay barn as the horses were all put to bed by the grooms. As the lights in the yard were turned off and the horses settled down to their munching, Lulu lay down under Blueberry's manger and dozed off. After a short while, however, Blueberry looked out over his stable door to see the grooms clattering out of their lodgings over the stables, the girls in glittery dresses and strange, high-heeled shoes, the boys in smart shirts and trousers, and they poured themselves into their cars with much laughter and shrieks before racing off down the drive.

82

"Party!" snorted Lulu, sleepily. "They won't be back for hours – better get some sleep kiddo, we'll both be woken up in the early hours of the morning when they finally get home."

Blueberry and Orange watched the lights of the cars disappear with interest. Blueberry supposed, having heard the excitement in their voices, the grooms were looking forward to their party as much as he looked forward to going to a competition. They worked hard and made sure he and his equine companions were well looked after so he hoped they would enjoy themselves. Carl hadn't gone with them, he noted. Lights were on in his house behind The Silver Dancer, and Blueberry could just see Carl in his office. It looked as though he still had work to do – there was no party for him.

It was only a couple of hours later when a car came through the Brook Mill gates and along the drive, triggering the security light that flooded the whole yard in brightness, causing all the horses to blink in the sudden glare. Lulu was up in an instant, wriggling through the hole at the back of Blueberry's stable and checking-out whoever could be arriving, unannounced, at this late time in the evening.

"Who is it?" asked Blueberry, as he watched his friend dash across the yard, her tail disappearing around the side of the archway and out into the car park. A flurry of furious barking filled the night air so that whoever had arrived in their car knew Lulu was in charge of security and onto them!

Moments later Carl arrived on the scene, his coat and Wellington boots over his pyjamas, headcollar in hand, followed by several people from the car that Blueberry didn't recognise. Lulu and Willow hovered around, Lulu still growling crossly in protest at the late hour, while Carl fastened a headcollar onto Uti.

"I did tell you he was lame," Carl explained, leading a hopping Uti out onto the yard.

Orange snorted and retreated back inside his stable in case Carl decided he might be next, but Blueberry, along with all the other horses in the yard, stared at the scene before him. What a strange thing to do in the middle of the night! Was this some Christmas tradition he didn't know about? The strangers all huddled around Uti and looked at his lame leg, whispering, tut-tutting and shaking their heads. Carl stood back and left them to it and Blueberry called over to Lulu.

"Whatever is going on?" he asked.

"I'll tell you later," growled Lulu, still keeping her one eye firmly on the strangers. Yes, she thought, that's exactly what they'd like her to do, take her concentration off them. But she

84

was wise to it. She wasn't going to take her eye off them for a second because if she did, Lulu was convinced that would be the moment they would do something they shouldn't. Not for nothing was Lulu head of Brook Mill security!

Finally, after a lot of discussion, Uti's rope was handed back to a shivering Carl, the muttering strangers all got back into their car, started the engine, turned it around and headed off down the drive, through the gates and out on to the road. Patting Uti's neck, Carl returned him to his stable, had a quick walk around the yard to make sure everyone else was okay and not upset by the visitors, switched all the lights out and walked back across the lawn, past The Silver Dancer, still glowing red, green and amber, and into the house, Willow firmly by his side.

Lulu slithered back into Blueberry's stable, still growling under her breath.

"Well?" asked Blueberry, impatient to learn about the mysterious visitors.

"I'm so mad, I can hardly speak about it," said Lulu, circling several times before flopping back down onto the Lulu-sized dent she had left in the wood chippings under Blueberry's manger, and letting out a long, furious sigh.

Blueberry said nothing. If his friend wanted to tell him, she would in her own time. Sure enough, after another couple of heavy sighs, Lulu began.

"You know Roly is your half-sharer," she said. Blueberry nodded, wondering what that had to do with anything. Roly shared him with Carl, he liked her, she helped to ensure he stayed with Carl and could continue his career as a top dressage horse. She often came to shows and watched him – she'd been at Olympia and had come around to his stable and given him some apples. She had also been in the arena when he'd been presented with his rosette and sash when he'd won. Roly was pretty cool.

"Well Uti has a sharer, too," explained Lulu. "And after his success in the European Championships in Rotterdam, his half-sharer was offered a lot of money to sell him to a rider who wanted a really good horse so they could ride and compete him. They want him now so they can compete in the Olympics with him for another country."

Blueberry felt his heart dip. Uti go to someone else? Someone else to ride him, compete him? How could that be possible? Only Carl could ride Uti. Anything else was unthinkable! Besides, Carl had *trained* Uti. That was what made their partnership so special, just as Carl's partnership with Charlotte and himself, Blueberry, was so

86

special. Surely the other rider would want to train his or her own horse!

"Those people who came to see Uti tonight were the people who wanted to buy him," Lulu continued. "They had come to see him so they could decide whether they wanted him."

"And did they want him?" cried Blueberry, wondering whether he really wanted to hear the answer. What Lulu told him next had the potential to wreak havoc with his life – not to mention Uti's.

"They said they'd be back in the morning and give their answer then."

Blueberry's heart did a flip – and then flipped back again. The strangers *might* want to buy Uti – but equally, they might *not*. He had to hope they *wouldn't* want him. Uti belonged here, with Carl, with his friends. Who would Blueberry go to competitions with if Uti went? Carl was determined they should both be selected for London 2012 – to compete for Team GB. It was what they were training for, what they were competing for.

"Does that mean Uti and I have been selected to go to London next year, to compete in the Olympic Games?" he asked.

"No," said Lulu. "If you both keep doing as well as you have been it is likely – but the selectors haven't decided yet, it's too soon. But nobody can compete in the Games with a horse unless they, or someone else in their country, have owned it since the beginning of the year – and that's in only a few days' time. If Uti is going to another rider, he will need to go soon to meet the deadline. It's all very complicated. Plus," she added, "even if they did buy him, it doesn't mean they'll be selected for their country. They might not get on with him as well as Carl does. It's madness!"

Lulu's reasoning gave Blueberry hope that Uti would stay. But then he had another thought.

"Roly won't want to sell *me*, will she?" he asked, his voice trembling.

"No," said Lulu, firmly. "Absolutely not. Put that thought right out of your mind, kiddo. I've told you before, you're not going anywhere."

Blueberry let out the breath he had been holding. It hadn't occurred to him that he might yet leave Brook Mill, not now, not now he and Charlotte were winning competitions. Surely he would stay here for ever.

"We'll have to hope Uti stays." said Blueberry, shakily.

"We certainly will, kiddo," replied Lulu. "That's all we can do. Meanwhile Uti – and everyone else – has to get through this night of uncertainty. I don't suppose anyone will get much sleep."

88

Blueberry returned to his haynet. He had to keep up his strength – and keep himself warm. Lulu watched him, her heart heavy. She hoped she had reassured her friend, prevented him from worrying about the possibility of being sold – but the truth was she, and no-one else, could ever really be sure. If Blueberry worried about it, it could prevent him from performing at his best, and he might just be worrying for nothing. Putting her nose on her paws, Lulu thought of how Brook Mill would be without Uti. They all had a long wait until morning, a long wait until the possibility that the strangers would return, having decided that they wanted to buy dressage success with Uti, and would be taking him away.

Chapter Eleven

When Blueberry awoke from his doze he knew immediately that something wasn't right. What was it? Then he remembered – Uti! The grooms had returned late, just as Lulu had predicted, but they didn't know that Uti's days at Brook Mill could be numbered. When they were told everyone was shocked, and morning stables were carried out in a subdued silence, with nobody wanting to talk about the possibility of losing one of the well-loved horses.

The morning dragged by. Every time Blueberry heard a vehicle coming along the drive his heart sank and he rushed to his door to see whether it brought the strangers, coming to take Uti away. But, thank goodness, each vehicle was known to them all.

Lunchtime came and went and the grooms ate very little. Still no strangers arrived. Blueberry's nerves were in shreds – he could only imagine how Uti must be feeling. Uti himself just kept his head in his stable and said nothing. His foot still hurt and he couldn't bring himself to talk to any of his friends on the yard. He knew they all supported him, and wanted him to stay.

Blueberry and Orange went for a hack. Some of the other horses had schooling sessions. In the afternoon, as usual, Carl taught his pupils in the outdoor arena and still nobody knew the outcome of the previous night's visit. Every time Carl's mobile phone rang everyone turned their heads to see whether he had received news – and Carl's mobile rang a lot! Each time it was someone else. It wasn't until late afternoon that Lulu had news.

"Carl's heard," she told Blueberry, her tail wagging, "and it's good news. They don't want to buy Uti, they think his lameness may take too long to heal and they don't want to chance buying a horse they can't immediately start preparing to qualify for the Olympics. It seems to me," Lulu added, "that fate has intervened.

91

Uti couldn't have chosen a better time to go lame!"

Blueberry felt as though a huge weight had been lifted from his heart. Uti was staying! Blueberry was overjoyed. He'd been worried sick.

There had been a time when Blueberry had been jealous of Uthopia. The little brown horse had wanted Carl to be his partner in competitions, but Carl had elected to ride Uti, and compete with him – rather than Blueberry who so idolised him. Resentment for Uti had filled Blueberry's heart, even though he had known it wasn't Uti's fault. It had taken him a while to overcome his envy, but overcome it he had. Now Blueberry loved being ridden by Charlotte, and was content for Carl to train them both. Neither Blueberry nor his rider could have been so successful without Carl, and his support and guidance. Thinking back, Blueberry found it difficult to understand how he had felt so badly towards his Uti, and was thankful they were friends. The thought that Carl might ride him if Uti were sold hadn't even entered his head. He had truly moved on from his jealous feelings and he felt he had grown up somewhat in the process. Thank goodness Uti was staying!

Carl soon told everyone on the yard and there was a collective sigh of relief. There would have been far more celebrations if the grooms hadn't been suffering from the effects of the previous night's party. Blueberry had noticed that they were not quite their usual, efficient selves and water buckets were checked twice, sometimes three times, wheelbarrows leant crookedly against walls, haynets taken ages to fill.

"They never learn," said Lulu, "but they'll be back to normal tomorrow. Thank goodness Christmas comes around only once a year! At least the ones who drove have their wits about them, they are no doubt glad now that they volunteered to drive."

Blueberry couldn't imagine why driving helped the grooms feel better after a party, but it seemed to be the case.

The excitement of the day wasn't over. That afternoon, just as everything seemed to be back to normal (if you didn't count the wobbly grooms), the weather went all strange.

"Hey, Blueberry," said Orange, giving his loud, throaty snort Blueberry knew to mean something out of the ordinary was happening, "whatever do you make of this?"

Looking out over his top door, Blueberry saw tiny flecks of white swirling down from the sky. As he watched, the tiny flecks got bigger and bigger, until big, fluffy flakes whirled past his door and settled on the ground.

"Snow!" barked Lulu, snapping at the flakes. Willow just looked at the snow falling down around him and licked all the ones which landed on his nose. Snowflakes settled on the big dog's back and head, until he looked as though someone had dusted him with sugar.

"It tickles!" gasped Blueberry, poking his head out over his door and feeling the snowflakes landing on his forelock, his face and his nose. The flakes were cold and the ones on his nose melted. He had seen snow before, but these flakes were much bigger than any he had seen in previous winters, and they seemed to be joining up and covering the ground in an alarming way.

"What does this mean?" groaned Orange, shaking. "Is it the end of the world? What can we do?"

Blueberry spotted Bonnie jumping up and trying to catch the snowflakes in her paws before rushing out of the yard with her tail up like a flag, deciding that the hay barn was a much better place than anywhere outside with all the wet whiteness. Clyde was way ahead of her, already watching from the warmth of the haystack, his legs and tail tucked under him in such a way that he looked as though he had neither, his eyes half-closed in the superior way cats have perfected. 'Snow' his demeanour

94

seemed to say, 'was not something in which cats should show any interest.'

The yard was soon covered in snowflakes, giving it a deep carpet of white, and the grooms hurried about to finish evening stables. As fast as they made footprints, the falling snowflakes filled them up again so the whole yard remained white. Alan picked up a handful of snow, patted it with the other hand and hurled it at one of the students. A snowball fight followed, with snowballs flying across the yard accompanied by shrieks and shouts until someone suggested they ought to take it to the outside arena where it wouldn't upset the horses.

Blueberry hadn't minded – except when a snowball whizzed past his ear and hit the back wall of his stable with a thud, breaking back into snow again as it slid down the wall. Willow frantically bounced about trying to catch the snowballs until he was successful. Then his face took on an expression of total surprise when all he got was a mouthful of snow, causing him to shake his head in disgust and spit it all out, confused. Even Lulu joined in, barking, returning to Blueberry's stable soaking wet and shivering when the grooms had had their fun, deciding that a warm fire was preferable to a wet, soggy, cold arena and wet, soggy and cold clothes.

"That was quite a laugh," said Lulu, licking her paw pads to melt the slithers of ice between them. "Quite took me back to my puppy days. There's still life in the old dog, yet," she said quietly, seemingly to herself.

"It's cold, this snow," said Blueberry, "but very pretty. And even though it's now night time, it isn't really dark. I can see all down the drive and out onto the fields. The snow makes everywhere lighter. How long will it be here?"

"Hard to tell," said Lulu, looking at the sky through Blueberry's half-door. "I can't see the stars which means the cloud is still there, and there could be much more snowfall before morning. We'll just have to see."

"Can I still go out in the field?" asked Blueberry, looking at how The Silver Dancer's lights were reflected on the bluey-white grass around him. Someone had put a huge tree with lights all over it outside Carl's house, and they twinkled in the darkness as though they were magic. Through one of the windows, Blueberry could see fairy lights on another, much smaller tree *inside* the house. Blueberry didn't know why Carl had a tree in his house at Christmas, but it looked very pretty.

"If the snow is still soft you probably can," said Lulu, satisfied that her paws were clear of ice. She rolled about in some of Blueberry's dropped hay to dry her coat and caught sight of his disappointed expression as he watched her.

Blueberry was less than impressed. It was his hay – his for the eating of, not Lulu's for rolling about in. He didn't fancy it now it was all doggified. Still, he supposed he could spare some of it for his best friend.

"If it freezes tonight, things will be tricky tomorrow," Lulu continued. "Frozen ground is rock hard and you can't see whether the ground below the snow is rutted. A horse can sprain a fetlock on frozen ground. Luckily, we have the indoor arena, which means all the horses can still be ridden, schooled and exercised."

"Will you be off on one of your epic sniff-a-thons later tonight?" asked Blueberry knowing that Lulu liked nothing more than disappearing into the darkness to check out all the smells in the surrounding area.

"Probably not. This snow is a bit deep for a short-legged dog," Lulu explained. "I'll give it a miss tonight."

As Blueberry munched his hay he could see the snow still floating gently down in the darkness outside his stable door. Everything seemed quieter in the snowfall. Everywhere seemed cloaked in a muffled whiteness. The cold seemed to hover in the air and Blueberry could see his breath coming out of his nose in clouds. Glad of his thick rug, Blueberry thought how lucky he was to be in his nice warm stable. Even so, he hoped he would be able to go out in the snow tomorrow, and feel it for himself.

Chapter Twelve

Orange stood by the field gate, his legs trembling, watching Blueberry rolling over and over and over in the snow. The cloud cover had remained, the snow – and the ground beneath it – hadn't frozen solid, and Blueberry and Orange had been turned out to enjoy themselves. And they did. Once Orange discovered he could walk, trot and canter, even though he couldn't see below his fetlocks for whiteness, he lost no time doing all three, putting in a buck and a leap for good measure.

The snow was cold and it tickled his legs and when Blueberry got up from rolling, Orange could see he had snow all over one side of his face, turning him into a skewbald.

"Try it!" said Blueberry, shaking from his nose to his tail so that snow flew up and away from his neck and rug like white dust. "It's weird, rolling in snow. Cold but refreshing."

And Orange had tried it, and when the grooms took them back in their stables after an hour or so, he still had tiny icicles in his mane, which knocked together as he walked, making a tinkling sound like bells.

"It's Christmas Eve," said Lulu. "Tomorrow is Christmas Day so things will be a bit different on the yard."

"How?" asked Blueberry, glad that Alan had replaced his waterproof outdoor rug with his cosy indoor duvet.

"Wait and see!" said Lulu, mysteriously, and Blueberry noticed everyone went home early that day – even the grooms who lived above the stables disappeared – leaving Carl and a few friends who were staying with him over Christmas to skip out the stables, check the rugs and water buckets and drinkers, give out the evening feeds and hang the haynets – amidst much laughter and questions about what went where and which horse was which.

"I'll be round later," Carl called over his

shoulder to the horses as he went back to the house with his friends. Lulu went with him, knowing there was a good possibility of some treats in the offing, especially from Carl's friends who were apt to spoil the dogs due to their novelty value. There was bound to be a warm lap to sit on, and the odd tasty morsel slipped from an unguarded plate.

Blueberry looked up at the sky. It was a clear night, the stars twinkled against the navy-blue expanse of sky and a silvery moon shone down, throwing shadows on the yard and highlighting the bushy, glittering cats' tails hanging from the doors. Clyde slipped past without a sound, his own tail low. He was in hunting mode, thought Blueberry, with a shudder. He couldn't understand the cats' obsession with chasing small furry animals. He could see the guinea fowl all hunched up in a line on the fence and wondered whether they felt the cold. The temperature had dropped – what had Lulu told him about cloud cover? The clouds had gone so no wonder it was colder.

One of the stars moved across the sky. It was bigger and brighter than the others. Another moved across in the opposite direction and Blueberry wondered where the stars were going, and where they came from. Why did stars move about, why didn't they bump into each other

101

– and where did they go in the morning when the sun arrived? Perhaps they weren't allowed to share the sky, perhaps they had to take it in turns – although he had sometimes seen the moon, pale and apologetic, during daylight hours.

Blueberry sighed. He had so many questions about the world and he doubted he would ever know all the answers, no matter how long he lived for. Even Lulu didn't know everything. He had come to realise that when she had responded to some of his questions with a shake of her head, or had told him he didn't need to know the answers.

"Perhaps it's better not to know everything," thought the little brown horse. "Maybe knowing everything is too mind-boggling. I don't think my brain is big enough to hold information about *everything* and I need it to hold all the information I *do* need. Like how to pirouette and how to do my tempi-changes, that's what's important. But sometimes, when I look up at the stars I do wonder. How much more is there to know?"

The little brown horse thought some more, and still more and was so tired when he had finished thinking that he fell asleep, his head low, a hind leg resting. He didn't even hear Lulu when she made her way back into his stable and joined him in sleep.

Carl and his house guests came out early the next morning and wished all the horses a Happy Christmas. They then got to work feeding, watering and mucking out.

"The grooms are all having the next couple of days off," explained Lulu, seeing the surprise on Blueberry's face when his bed wasn't mucked out in *quite* the right way.

"I'm not complaining, don't think I am…" said Orange, looking sideways at his water bucket which had been put back in the wrong corner, "… but I'm starting to feel quite anxious. With my water bucket there, instead of here, it feels like my stable is the wrong way around. I'm feeling sort of woozy."

"I think I've got *your* water bucket, Blueberry," said Uti. "Mine isn't this colour."

"I don't think I've got yours…" said Blueberry, giving it a good look, "…I don't know who this belongs to but like yours, Orange, it's in the wrong corner. I'll have to walk around my stable if I want to dunk my hay in it."

"It's only for two days, the grooms will be back soon," said Lulu. "You can put up with it for two days, can't you?"

Blueberry remembered that previous Christmases had been similar – the grooms going for two days, Carl's friends helping out instead. It was different!

Everyone agreed that they could put up with it – but then Carl did a quick check, looking over everyone's half-doors and rearranged the water buckets so that Orange felt calm again and Blueberry could dunk with ease. But then the tack was brought out and all the horses were soon tacked up and ready for some exercise.

"Uh-oh," said Orange. "I don't like the look of this."

"I'm still on box rest." Uti said smugly, although his foot seemed, thankfully, to be on the mend.

But they had nothing to worry about – all Carl's friends were expert horsemen and women – and, with all their strange riders on board, the horses headed out for a Christmas hack in the woods, the snow still on the ground and clinging to the trees. The temperature had risen sharply and Blueberry could hear the drip, drip, drip of melting snow as it plopped from branches, peppering the snow around his hooves with tiny black holes as though some strange creature had galloped through the snow in the night. He could feel the ground beneath the snow give under his hooves, so it wasn't frozen and dangerous.

Sticking to the paths they knew, the whole party had a great time – especially the riders who weren't familiar with their mounts and were sometimes taken by surprise when the horses displayed their usual cheeky characteristics. Orange almost unseated his rider when he shied at something he thought he had seen – even though he hadn't – and Blueberry felt his own heart lift in an inward smile as Carl and the other riders all laughed. They all set off at a canter – which got faster and faster as the horses caught the excitement of the moment.

"This isn't a horse!" cried Blueberry's rider, as they cantered up alongside Carl. "It's a rubber ball. I can't even sit to his canter!"

"You're riding a future star there," laughed Carl. "You'll look back on this day and remember riding our Blueberry!"

When they got back to the yard all the horses were rugged up, watered and fed, and Carl and his houseguests disappeared into the house, leaving the horses to their peace and quiet. Blueberry noticed Bonnie and Clyde return. Upset by the unfamiliar voices, they had fled the yard. Now things had quietened down they were back, but clearly missing their usual humans.

The snow had almost gone by the time Carl and his guests did evening stables. There was much laughter and joking, but again Carl checked that all the horses had exactly what they needed – in the right place – when everyone had finished.

"I said Christmas was bonkers, didn't I?" said Lulu. "We won't be back to normal until the day after tomorrow."

"I don't mind," said Blueberry. "It makes a change and everyone is so happy."

"It's quite unsettling," said Orange.

"I think it's interesting," said Blueberry. He and Orange always had been like chalk and cheese. Orange was suspicious of anything new; Blueberry was interested.

"It wouldn't do for us all to be the same," said Lulu.

No, thought Blueberry, it wouldn't.

"It will soon be the start of a new year," said Lulu. "2011 is almost gone and in a few days' time we'll be welcoming in the year 2012. It's customary for everyone to make a New Year's Resolution, you know. What will yours be, Blueberry?"

Because of the passing of the seasons, Blueberry understood about the how years worked. He was nine years old now, and in the summer of next year he'd be ten. He hadn't realised the year began after Christmas, or about New Year's resolutions. What did that mean, exactly?

"What will your New Year's resolution be, Lulu?" he asked, hoping his friend's answer would give him an idea of what it might be about.

"Easy," said Lulu. "My New Year's resolution is to go to more shows with you, Blueberry, and to ensure I don't miss out on any snacks which might be in the offing – particularly with the grooms."

Blueberry understood a little more how resolutions worked and he knew exactly what his was going to be.

"My New Year's resolution," he began, solemnly, "is to be selected to compete with Charlotte at the 2012 Olympic Games in London."

Lulu nodded. "Of course," she said. "The way you're going, kiddo, I think that's one New Year's resolution that may just be in the bag!"

Blueberry didn't get the bag thing, but he realised that his resolution wasn't just a pie-in-the-sky dream. He had a real chance of making it come true, but he still had work to do.

Chapter Thirteen

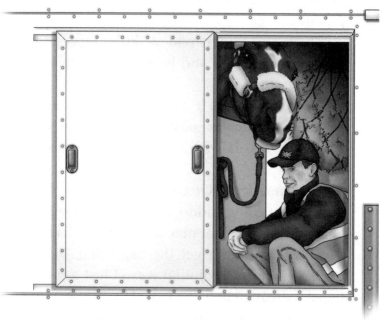

One morning some time after Christmas, after a schooling session that Blueberry had particularly enjoyed – he had felt the work he and Charlotte had put in to their lateral movements, and their pirouettes, had been especially successful – Blueberry saw Lulu dash out of Carl's house and rush over to his stable.

"Big news, kiddo," she said. "I just overheard Carl talking on the telephone. It seems you are going to the USA."

"What's that?" asked Blueberry.

"It's a country – a long way away. You'll have to fly there."

Blueberry felt his chin contract. He couldn't fly… or could he? After all, he hadn't always been able to pirouette, but he could now. How long would it take for Carl and Charlotte to teach him to fly?"

Lulu guessed what was going on in her friend's mind. "You'll go in a plane," she explained. "It's a flying machine – huge – just like a big horsebox that can fly. You've seen them in the sky. Remember?"

"Oh, those birds that don't flap their wings, are they planes?" asked Blueberry, remembering how he and Orange had looked up at them as they had passed over his field high, high up in the sky.

"They're the ones," said Lulu.

"Are they the stars that move across the sky at night?" asked Blueberry, in a sudden flash of inspiration.

"Yup – aeroplanes," agreed Lulu, glad she didn't have to explain any further. She didn't know very much about planes herself.

Blueberry could hardly contain his excitement. He was going to fly on one of the moving stars, an aeroplane. He hadn't realised they were big enough for him to go inside. He hoped he'd be able to look out and see Brook

Mill below him. That would be something! If Orange was out in the field, he might even be able to see him. He talked to Uti about it, but Uti surprised him.

"I'm not going," he said.

"But your foot is okay now." said Blueberry.

"I know, but Carl is going to ride his friend's horse. He doesn't think I'll travel all that way very well and I don't really mind. You're a better traveller than I am, and I hope you do well."

As Blueberry was led up the ramp of the horsebox he heard Lulu, Orange and Uti shout their goodbyes and wish him good luck. He was so excited and couldn't wait to get on a plane, but he soon realised he wasn't travelling alone. A big chestnut with a tiny star and narrow snip, was waiting in the horsebox.

"Hello," cried Blueberry. "Who are you?"

"I'm Wie Atlantico, known as Wie," replied the chestnut. "My owner has asked Carl to ride me in a competition because she is having a baby."

Blueberry introduced himself and thought that Wie seemed a nice enough horse, and easy company. They both settled down to their haynets as Alan took to the road. But Blueberry soon realised that Alan was driving the horsebox towards Dover, where they crossed the channel – either on it by boat, or under it by tunnel –

110

to the Continent. What about the plane he was supposed to fly in?

"We're probably going from a Dutch airport," said Wie, who seemed very relaxed about it all, having flown before. When they got to the other side of the English Channel, via the tunnel, Alan drove on and on, occasionally stopping to check that Blueberry and Wie were okay.

"Don't worry, we'll get to Schiphol airport soon," Alan told his passengers, and the little brown horse relaxed. He was going to fly after all – he was beginning to wonder whether Lulu had been winding him up! As they got closer to the airport, Blueberry could hear deep whooshing sounds and felt the horsebox tremble as the planes took off and landed, flying over the horsebox. And the planes were huge! Blueberry realised they could get many, many horseboxes inside them, just like the huge ferries did, provided they were all behind each other in a line. Planes were long and thin and ferries were wide.

What Blueberry didn't realise was that the actual horsebox wasn't going to the USA. As it came to a halt, Blueberry watched Alan unload all his and Wie's equipment, their tack, their rugs and grooming kits, bales of hay, feed and buckets, putting them all into another container which was then towed away. They were parked on a huge concrete area, and Blueberry could still hear and see the planes as they moved around the airport. There were uniformed people checking things and it all took quite a long while. Blueberry wondered when they would get going.

Eventually, Alan came to check that his special headcollar, with padding on the sides and across his poll to protect his head when he travelled, was on properly. He then led Blueberry down the ramp and towards another ramp which went into what looked like a trailer with a pair of stalls. Wie was next and the two were soon comfortable.

"Nothing to worry about," Alan told them – not that Blueberry had been worried. Alan was always very calm about everything and Blueberry took his cue from him. Alan wasn't going to leave his charge, however, and sat in the space under Blueberry's haynet, offering reassurance to the two horses.

Blueberry soon realised that they weren't actually in a trailer, the stalls were a crate which was pulled along by a small vehicle into the plane. Inside, Blueberry realised there wasn't as much room as he had thought – the horsebox would only just have fitted inside. His stall, like his stall in the horsebox, was compact, so he couldn't turn around or lie down. It was safer for him to stay upright in transit, rather than move around too much. Alan wriggled out from under his nose and he and Wie's groom had some chairs to sit on. Blueberry could hear them chatting while the two horses tugged at their hay.

Presently, the doors behind them closed and Blueberry heard the whine of the engines start up. It was loud, but not unbearable. Whenever he travelled on the ferry he could hear the throbbing of the engines, but this was different. This sound was pitched higher, and rather than the rolling motion of the sea beneath the boat's hull, the plane moved more like a horsebox. He couldn't help feeling disappointed; the crate had only the grooms' door at the front and no windows, so he couldn't see out. How would he see Brook Mill and Orange now?

"They do that on purpose," explained Wie, when he mentioned it. "They think we'll panic if we look out and see nothing but sky. They think we don't realise we're flying, but believe we're just in a horsebox. Honestly, how dim do they think we are?"

Blueberry wondered whether he would have imagined being able to fly if Lulu hadn't explained it to him. After all, he had thought the moving lights in the sky had been stars. He really should have realised they were the unflapping birds he saw in the sky during the day time.

The plane moved off and Blueberry could feel it trembling under his feet. Then the engine noise increased and he could tell that the plane was getting faster, much, much faster and then, all of a sudden, it seemed to do something else. Blueberry felt his forefeet were higher than his hind feet and altogether he felt strangely lighter.

"We're in the air," said Wie, matter-of-factly, between chews of his hay.

"Wow," said Blueberry. "I'm flying!"

It was a long trip. Alan made sure Blueberry had plenty of hay, with a bucket of water for him to dunk it in, as always. Both horses thought nothing of their mode of transport, even when the plane dipped and rolled a little through some turbulence. Blueberry's chin wobbled and his ears flicked back and forth. With Alan standing calmly by his side, he decided it was nothing to worry about and he made himself comfortable for the journey – however long it took.

Eventually, it was time to land and his water bucket was taken away as the plane gradually dropped through the air until it was lined up to land in Florida. Blueberry could feel the plan descending – it was as though the floor dropped away from his hooves a little. He felt a bump, heard the engines whine even louder, and

Blueberry felt himself thrown forward a little as the pilot reversed the engines to slow the plane down until it finally came to a halt.

Alan was back at Blueberry's head reassuring him, but the little brown horse was perfectly calm. It was amazing, he thought, wondering how many horses got to fly in an aeroplane.

When the doors opened, Blueberry was struck by the warmth of the temperature. Florida, USA, was a hot place! The horses were quickly transferred to another horsebox where Blueberry had a very long drink of water (his flight had left him strangely thirsty) and after all their – and the grooms' – papers had been checked, they were driven to Palm Beach where the World Dressage Masters competition was being held.

The venue was extraordinary. Talking with some of the other horses during exercise, Blueberry learned that most of the United States' equestrian competitors spent the winter there, taking advantage of the warm climate. It meant they weren't hampered by bad weather and the horses could relax in the sunshine. The contrast to the weather Blueberry had left behind at home was striking. No howling, biting wind. No freezing temperatures, no need for his thick, quilted rugs. And Alan enjoyed the contrast too – there were no freezing taps or muddy fields.

Everything was so much easier for everyone.

But Blueberry had a job to do – he wasn't on holiday. With Carl and Charlotte now there with him, the little horse was soon going over his movements for the class in which he was entered; the Grand Prix, and the final class he hoped to get a qualifying score for, the Grand Prix Special.

Chapter Fourteen

The Grand Prix was first and several factors put added pressure on the little brown horse and his rider. Firstly, Blueberry's recent successes hadn't escaped the attention of the American dressage enthusiasts, and the atmosphere around the arena was electric with anticipation. That the home crowd were rooting for their own favourite, the big dark bay stallion Ravel, with his distinctive, narrow lightning-flash of white down the middle of his face, and ridden by the top US rider Steffen Peters, only added to the atmosphere, which could be felt by everyone. How would the little brown horse from England, with a growing reputation but little experience and so far from home, fare at this level against seasoned competitors?

Blueberry felt the expectations of the crowd. Although he and Charlotte had warmed up and worked well before his Grand Prix he still felt full of energy, and couldn't wait to get in and show everyone what he was made of. As they began their test, Charlotte did all she could to calm her mount, but he was hot and keen, and his keenness resulted in a couple of big mistakes to give them a score of just over 78 percent. Big mistakes there may have been, but the pair still stood second to Ravel, which said something about the quality of the rest of their test.

Blueberry was disappointed in himself. He had to control his exuberance! He had thrown away those marks and if he had just kept it together he might have won. Carl and Charlotte didn't say so – but he knew it was the case. He didn't know that Carl was carefully planning his career so that he gained experience – and the mistakes he had made in his test were part of that learning curve.

Blueberry had done well enough in the Grand Prix to qualify for the Freestyle, and was determined not to blow it. He and Charlotte

118

performed a beautiful test, much appreciated by the knowledgeable crowd. Had they done enough to improve their placing in the Grand Prix and win the class?

Steffen Peters thought so – he congratulated Charlotte as she steered Blueberry out of the arena and waited for her marks. Blueberry was walking on air – he had done it; he had proved he was better than his last test. He was delighted to have pleased Carl and Charlotte so much and he gave his now customary nod to the crowd on his way out.

Dressage marks are given by individual judges, all placed at different places around the arena so that each sees the riders and horses from a different perspective. With such close marks between the top riders and horses, every percentage point mattered. Blueberry and Charlotte's mark was an impressive 83.65 percent, but just one lower mark can have a huge impact on the overall score and so it was in Blueberry's Grand Prix Freestyle; just one judge preferred Ravel's test to Blueberry's and it was this single score that put Blueberry once again behind Ravel to stand second by only the smallest of margins.

It was disappointing, but Blueberry saw how Carl and Charlotte were philosophical about it. There was no use getting despondent, the judges were there to do a difficult job and they scored how they saw fit. Carl was just thrilled that Blueberry had performed so well and he was always thinking of the long-term plan for his team. London 2012 was well and truly in sight for the little brown horse. He hadn't put a hoof wrong and, with the Olympics only eight months away, Carl could see no reason for the selectors not to consider him for the team. The dream was still intact, still possible – and getting more probable with every competition.

The excitement of Florida wasn't over. Blueberry and Charlotte went back into the arena for the prize giving, where something happened which was totally out of character for the little horse. With his prize-winning sash around his neck Blueberry stood with the other horses, waiting for the moment when they would canter around in a lap of honour. Blueberry always enjoyed it when the crowd clapped and Charlotte was relaxed and happy. But as they were waiting another of the horses, excited and flustered, became unsettled, his rider unable to control him, and he bounced into Blueberry. It was the last thing the little horse expected and, feeling threatened, he reacted instinctively, rearing on his hind legs like a film horse for the first and only time in his life.

Quickly coming back down to earth,

120

Blueberry felt ashamed. Why had he done that? He couldn't understand it. For a horse which was so used to the unusual he had been caught off-guard, and he vowed he would never do anything so ill-mannered again. He remembered something Lulu had about being bumped into and wondered whether he was now famous enough for the other horse to have bumped into him on purpose. If that was the case, Blueberry didn't enjoy it and wasn't impressed. He hoped it wasn't going to happen anywhere else. What must Charlotte think of him? He felt her reassure him, hoping he wasn't too upset, unaware of how much he regretted his behaviour. Thank goodness she didn't blame him, he thought. He just had to make sure it never happened again, whatever the behaviour of the other horses. He was above that, he decided!

"How was Germany. Hagen wasn't it?" asked Lulu several weeks later.

"Amazing!" replied Blueberry. "After Florida, Carl wanted Charlotte and me to get experience at Hagen in our Grand Prix Freestyle – you know, the test where we do all the Grand Prix movements, but freestyle them to fit with our music. Apparently, the scores when we do that test at the Olympics will be crucial for individual medals."

121

"I understand you exceeded everyone's expectations." said Lulu. She knew how well Blueberry had performed at Hagen, and was impressed that he wasn't shouting it from the rooftops. The little horse had learned his lesson about humility well. But still, Lulu knew, it didn't do any harm to be excited about a good result and it was important to celebrate successes.

"It was fantastic," sighed Blueberry, thinking back to the *Horses and Dreams* show in Hagen. It had been such a lovely show and he had heard Carl telling Charlotte that they would be up against many horses and riders who would be at the Olympic Games, so it was important to see how they fared against them.

"Tell me about it, then," said Lulu.

"We won the Grand Prix with a score of 81 percent," began Blueberry. "I didn't think things could get any better than that, we were all very pleased about it. But it was the Grand Prix Special which was totally amazing. I hope this doesn't sound big-headed, Lulu, but I don't remember making any mistakes in that test at all. The judges thought so, too. We got a huge score of 88 percent. I could hardly believe it!"

"A new world record for the Special, I believe," said Lulu, "a whole two percent higher than the previous record. You should be very proud of yourself."

"The crowd gave us a standing ovation," Blueberry continued, staring out of his stable but seeing only himself back in Hagen, the crowd all around him, clapping, cheering and calling his name. "That's what you call it when they all stand up to clap," he explained.

"It's very special," agreed Lulu. "Very few people get a standing ovation."

"I could feel how emotional Charlotte was at the prize-giving – she had been speechless when she'd seen the scores. She was holding back the tears, as was Carl. Alan was welling up, too. Everyone was in pieces. I got a lovely rosette – it's in the tack room – and a sash, and the Germans have the right idea when they give out the prizes because I got some carrots, too, which were much nicer than the rosette and sash, to be honest."

"I've got some other great news for you," said Lulu, unable to keep it to herself any longer. "I overheard Carl on the telephone just now – you and Uti have both been selected for the Olympics later this year. You've done it, kiddo, you're going to be an Olympic horse!"

Blueberry hadn't thought he could ever feel better than he had when his score of 88 percent at Hagen had been announced, and he had known he had set a new World Record. But as Lulu's words sunk in he realised that his career as a dressage horse offered him countless possibilities to improve his performance, to go on to greater things with Carl and Charlotte. He had been selected for the Olympics. His dream was coming true.

"Carl is coming to tell everyone," said Lulu, seeing Carl running across the lawn, past The Silver Dancer, towards the yard.

Blueberry followed her gaze. He had achieved his ambition to dance like The Silver Dancer and still there were more challenges to meet. How many more of his dreams could come true?

Coming Soon…

Don't miss the next exciting book in *The Blueberry Stories*, when Blueberry fulfils his dream to compete with Charlotte at the Olympic Games in London!

Blueberry extras

Don't ride now and again

When you watch a good rider compete in dressage it can seem as though they are not doing much, and that the horse is doing it all by himself. That's the image everyone is aiming for – invisible aids so that the pair becomes one. But you don't need to be a top dressage rider to ride like that.

It is easy to think that riders who seem to just sit there have horses which are easy to ride. The chances are, the rider is correcting every move the horse does that they haven't asked for, and are working all the time to produce a smooth, regular gait and good transitions. Their horse is likely to be just as tricky as yours – changing pace, deviating from a straight line and all those things horses do because they have no incentive to do otherwise. No horse walks straight and at a regular pace unless the rider asks them to.

The trick is to ride *all the time* – but don't mistake this with nagging. A nagging rider legs the horse continually until the horse switches off. It becomes background noise to be ignored. A rider who rides all the time knows what they want and asks for it – and they make corrections.

The dialogue between horse and rider may go something like this:

You're going too slow, no that's a little too fast, this is the pace I want (relax aids).

You're going too fast, you're going too slow, you're not using enough energy, this is just right (relax aids).

You're wobbling to the left, straighten up – not too far to the right, straighten up, now you're going just right (relax aids).

When you are aware of every little deviation your horse makes, and you can correct it so that anyone watching you sees only your horse walking at a regular pace, in a straight line, you are on the way to riding like a dressage rider.

Judging discrepancies

Everyone who takes part in dressage, in which your score is decided by the opinion of judges, accepts that there are bound to be times when they feel they have been judged less than fairly.

But here's the thing: human beings hold different views on almost everything, and the judges would find it impossible if their task was to please everyone rather than to mark what they see. The only way of pleasing everyone is to place everyone first – and we all know that can't, and shouldn't, happen! Dressage judges receive a lot of training to ensure standards are as high as possible but even so they may still hold their own views on what they think is right in dressage movements – which they mark higher – and what they think is not so good – for which they give lower marks.

Top dressage is marked by a team of judges, all placed around the arena, so that each judge sees a different view of the same horse and rider combination, which is why sometimes the marks can vary slightly. This is the fairest way because each rider is fully aware of their own and their horse's weaknesses, and could attempt to conceal these from a judge placed at only one part of the arena.

If you get disappointing marks in dressage then I would advise you to read the comments given on your sheet to explain your marks. They are there to help you and enable you to work on your weaknesses. You'll find each judge has their own pet hates and dislikes but overall, the comments are your worksheet for future schooling.

In our sport, disappointments are bound to happen – a dropped percentage point here and there can make a huge difference to an overall score and eventual placing. But remember that for every dropped percentage point you get one day, you may make up the next with a generous gift point!

If you're the sort of person who can't accept that judges are human then you may wish to change your sport to one where subjective judging doesn't take place – show jumping, for example. There is no margin for ambiguity there, as four faults are clear for everyone to see!

A Brook Mill Christmas

Christmas at Brook Mill is always a time for everyone to chill and for the staff to enjoy some time off with their own families. I usually have a full house of guests during Christmas, and everyone invited knows they're expected to muck in – and out – with the horses. Nobody minds. In fact, everyone enjoys it. With the big Christmas show at Olympia now such a big date in the dressage calendar, things are extra busy just before Christmas, and the yard is quite frantic what with social occasions to squeeze in and all the usual winter work to get through. Bad weather just makes it that much more difficult!

Of course, however much we love a bit of rest and relaxation over the festive period, the horses still need not only looking after, but

129

exercising as well. They go out in the field to chill, and sometimes the guests (if they're good enough riders) are up for a hack out with me. The horses sometimes like to show off a bit with their unsuspecting riders – after all, it's their Christmas, too!

Alan the Supergroom!

Alan came to Brook Mill after Blueberry's previous groom left to become a veterinary nurse. It's always sad to say goodbye to someone who is brilliant at their job and has become an integral part of our team, but everyone has their own destiny to follow. I already knew Alan so I knew he would be perfect for our Blueberry, who was headed for stardom.

Alan is what we call a *Supergroom*. He's totally dedicated to Blueberry, and sees to his every need, going the extra mile to ensure he has every comfort and is totally relaxed at home and away. He's quite protective of him, actually, and doesn't like anyone else looking after his baby.

I couldn't run my operation at Brook Mill without people like Alan. It's not just about the work they do caring for the horses, it's also about knowing that they share my philosophy about them and want not only the best for their charges, but will go the extra mile for them. Looking after horses is not like any other job; with horses that compete at weekends, late at night and all over the world, work for the people who look after them becomes their life. Quite apart from the fact that the horses are family to us, the grooms are caring for animals worth many millions of pounds. The horses are top-class athletes, but they're also our partners and we always want the best for them. That means getting the best people to care for them – and Alan is up there with the very best.

Are you in control?

Everyone knows when their horse or pony is going too fast. Going too fast means the rider is out of control! But if your horse or pony goes slower than you want him to, if he chooses the pace – and that pace is slower than you have asked for – then the rider is just as much out of control as if their horse were bolting at a gallop! Not so scary, but still *out of control*.

The rider should always choose the pace, not the horse. Otherwise, horses and ponies know that if their rider allows them to go too slow, then they can certainly go too fast! Ask yourself when you ride, is my horse or pony going at the pace I have chosen, or one at which he has decided? Who's riding whom?

Admin, admin, admin...

Administration work for any national or international competition horse is a full-time job – and when you have as many horses as I have, it can take over your life. Luckily, I have a great personal assistant, Claudine, who takes on a lot of the stress involved on the paperwork side. I'm probably the worst person you would employ to deal with admin! I'm always forgetting the rules and regulations, and if I didn't have Claudine, we'd all end up at shows we hadn't entered for, and horses without the necessary paperwork.

Not only do the horses have all their own admin to consider but we have plenty of other things going on at Brook Mill to give anyone without an admin-head a breakdown! Sponsors and horse owners need to be kept up-to-date to ensure they are happy with how their horses are progressing. I'm asked to charity events, we have demonstrations and visits at Brook Mill to organise and book signings to fit in, not to mention all the lessons and visits from the farrier, equine dentist, the physio and all the other people essential to running a dressage yard. If I had to do all that, I'd never get any time in the saddle!

If you enjoyed reading this book you may want to answer these questions or discuss them with your friends or class at school:

Chapter 1

1) We know that Blueberry misses Lulu, why do you think she doesn't travel abroad?
2) *"But Carl says we make our own luck,"* Blueberry had said. *"He says the harder we work, the luckier we become because we leave nothing to chance."* Can you think of one way in which Carl, Charlotte and Blueberry each work hard to ensure nothing is left to chance?

Chapter 2

1) Do you think Orange knew who Wim Ernes was? If not, why didn't he ask Blueberry?
2) Why do you think Blueberry was glad that Clyde asked him who Wim Ernes is?

Chapter 3

1) Blueberry is described as... *'staring... but not noticing...'*. What do you think he saw in his mind's eye at that time?
2) Can you match the word to the definition? Use the text around the words to help if you are unsure.

134

WORD	DEFINITION
equine	a box or trough in a stable or barn from which horses or cattle eat
manger	relating to the diseases, injuries, and treatment of farm and domestic animals
mastiff	of, relating to, or resembling a horse or the horse family
presence	the immediate proximity of someone or something
veterinary	a dog of a large, strong breed with drooping ears and a smooth coat

Chapter 4

1) *'The hands stroking his neck were obviously used to horses...'*. What do you think it was that Blueberry noticed as Alan stroked his neck?
2) *'...putting her paw firmly onto Blueberry's woes...'* What is it that Lulu is actually managing to do?

Chapter 5

1) What important concept does Blueberry learn from Uthopia in this chapter?
2) Why are Orange's eyes compared to saucers? What does the use of this simile tell you about Orange's reaction to seeing the vet arrive?

Chapter 6

1) Whilst in Rotterdam, Blueberry spends much of his time remembering his friends and the good life he has at home in Brook Mill. This makes him more confident and more determined to succeed. How do you think Orange would react to memories of home?

2) What important concept does Blueberry remember learning from Lulu in this chapter?

Chapter 7

1) Which countries' teams eventually won the gold, silver and bronze medals in the Team Grand Prix?

2) *'Standing with an emotional Alan behind the podium,..'*. List at least three emotions that Alan might be feeling at that moment.

Chapter 8

1) Why do you think Carl believes *'It was unrealistic to expect perfect performances every time'*?

2) '…passing The Silver Dancer still and serene as always on the lawn…'. What do you think serene means?

Chapter 9

1) What do you think made the *'bangs and pops'* that kept the animals awake one night?
2) At Olympia, Blueberry recognised some of the horses with him in Rotterdam (chapter six). Do you think any of them would mock him this time? Explain your reasoning.

Chapter 10

1) Why do think the grass doesn't taste particularly good in December?
2) If Uti had to leave Brook Mill, what would Blueberry miss most about him?

Chapter 11

1) What are the two reasons that the Brook Mill staff are particularly quiet on this morning?
2) Why do you think *'Everything seemed quieter in the snowfall.'*?

Chapter 12

1) Had you expected Orange to play and roll in the snow? If so, explain why. If not, what had you expected him to do instead?
2) Brook Mill staff have two days off for

Christmas and Carl's friends are happy to take on their duties. What does that tell you about Carl's relationship with his staff? What does this also tell you about Carl's relationship with his friends?

Chapter 13
1) How do you think Blueberry might have felt if Lulu hadn't explained 'flying' to him?
2) Do you think Wie was a good travelling companion for Blueberry? Use quotations from the text to support your thoughts.

Chapter 14

1) In this chapter, we hear about many people's reactions to Blueberry's recent success and his good news. What do you think Lydia would say to him if she was there?
2) Lulu and Uti have often shared their wisdom and experience with Blueberry. Can you think of one key piece of advice from each of these two friends that will help Blueberry as he begins his preparation for the Olympics?

Glossary of equestrian terms introduced in Book Four

Cadre Noir

The Cadre Noir is an equestrian display team based in the city of Saumur in western France. The troop was founded in 1828, and gets its name from the black uniforms that are still used today. It is one of the most prestigious horsemanship schools in the world

Cobby (hooves)

Slightly larger and rounder than 'normal' hooves, considered to be stronger and traditionally more able to carry larger amounts of weight

Competition

Dressage competitions consist of a series of individual tests with an increasing level of difficulty. The most accomplished horse and rider teams perform FEI tests. The highest level of modern competition is at Grand Prix level. This is the level of test ridden in the prestigious international competitions (CDI's), such as the Olympic Games,

Dressage World Cup, and World Equestrian Games

Defra

The Department for Environment, Food and Rural Affairs (Defra) is the government department responsible for environmental protection, food production and standards, agriculture, fisheries and rural communities in the United Kingdom

Diagonal (legs)

At a trot or similar movement, the set of legs that move forward at the same time are the diagonal pair e.g. left foreleg and right hindleg

Diagonal (direction)

In dressage, a line crossing the centre of the arena running from one end corner (quarter marker) or long side to the opposite end corner, quarter marker or long side

FEI

The *Féd*ération Équestre Internationale or International Federation for Equestrian Sports (FEI) is the governing body for most international-level equestrian competitions, including the FEI World Equestrian Games and the Olympics. It recognises and governs ten disciplines: dressage, combined driving, endurance riding, eventing, horseball, para-equestrian, reining, show jumping, tent pegging, and equestrian vaulting. The FEI does not govern horse racing or polo.

Fetlock

The joint on the lower leg, above the hoof, below the knee or hock

Flying changes in sequence

Informally called 'tempis' or 'tempi changes' at Grand Prix level. The horse changes leads of leg at the canter every stride (one-time tempis), two strides (two-time tempis), three strides or four strides

Freestyle (to music) or Kur

Sometimes known as Musical Kur or simply kur (from German *kür*, 'freestyle') this is a form of dressage competition where the required dressage movements for a particular level are set to music of the rider's choice to create a competitive 'dance' that best shows off the horse's ability. As well as the movements, it is judged and scored by the degree of difficulty, artistic choreography and interpretation of music

Grand Prix

In dressage, the highest level or test undertaken. It takes many years to train a horse to Grand Prix standard, and they must be at least eight years old before undertaking a Grand Prix test

Required movements for Grand Prix level dressage include:
Walk - Extended and Collected
Trot - Medium, Extended and Collected, Half Pass
Canter - Medium, Extended and Collected, Zig-Zag Half Pass and Multiple Flying Lead Changes Every one or two Strides,
Pirouettes
Piaffe, Passage
Halts - Collected Canter to Halt and Passage to Halt - immobility

Grand Prix Special

The Grand Prix Special is similar to the standard Grand Prix test and consists of Grand Prix movements arranged in a different, more difficult, pattern

Green (horse term)

A green horse or pony is one that is inexperienced, untrained or lightly trained.

142

The term is also used to describe riders who are similarly inexperienced or untrained. A horse can be well-trained at one level (e.g. novice level) but green at a new level (e.g. Grand Prix level)

Impulsion

Impulsion is the movement of a horse or pony when it is going forward with controlled power and can occur at the walk, trot and canter. Impulsion can only occur if the horse is working properly up through the back and hindquarters. Impulsion not only encourages correct muscle and joint use, but also engages the mind of the horse or pony, focusing it on the rider

Judges

Judges are registered through their national federation depending on the judge's experience and training, with the highest qualified being registered with the FEI for international competition. There is always a judge sitting at C, although for upper-level competition there can be up to seven judges at different places around the arena — at C, E, B, K, F, M, and H — which allows the horse to be seen in each movement from all angles. This helps prevent certain faults from going unnoticed, which may be difficult for a judge to see from only one area of the arena

Lateral movements

Lateral movements are when the horse or pony is moving in a direction other than straight forward (e.g. half-pass, shoulder-in, renvers, travers). They are used both in training and in competition and vary in difficulty

Locked–up (equine term)

Horses and ponies most frequently rest or sleep in a standing position. The 'stay apparatus' of the forelegs and 'check apparatus' (functions of the leg tendons and ligaments) of the hind legs allows them to rest and relax while not falling down. Resting a hind leg is often referred to as 'locked up'.

Poll

The poll is the area at the top of the head of a horse or pony right between and behind the ears. It is considered the highest point of a **horse** or pony, as the ears are not counted.

Skewbald (colour)

A horse or pony with patches of brown (or any other colour than black) and white colouring

144

Snip

A white marking on the muzzle, between the nostrils

Tests

Dressage tests are a number of dressage movements used in competition. Although horses and riders are competing against each other, tests are completed by one horse and rider combination at a time, and horses and riders are judged against a common standard, rather than having their performance scored in comparison to the other competitors.

Please see books One, Two and Three for a glossary of terms introduced in earlier parts of the story